DOUBLEDAY
CELEBRATES
100 YEARS OF
EXCELLENCE

Also by Jonathan Lethem

Gun, with Occasional Music

Amnesia Moon

The Wall of the Sky, the Wall of the Eye (stories)

As she climbed

Doubleday
New York London Toronto
Sydney Auckland

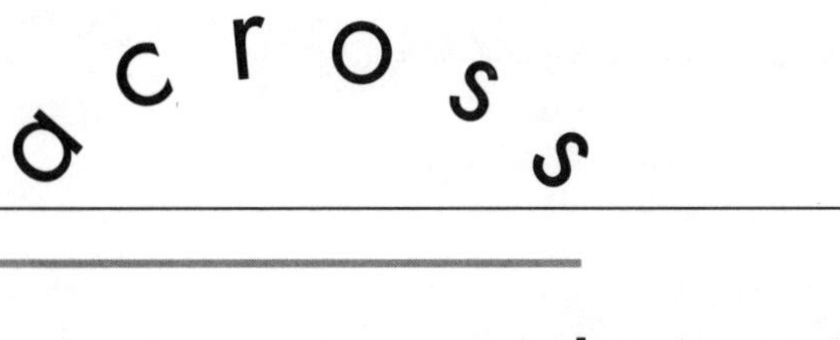

the table

PUBLISHED BY DOUBLEDAY
a division of Bantam Doubleday Dell Publishing Group, Inc.
1540 Broadway, New York, New York 10036

Book design by Maria Carella

Library of Congress Cataloging-in-Publication Data
Lethem, Jonathan.
As she climbed across the table / Jonathan Lethem. — 1st ed.
p. cm.
I. Title.
PS3562.E8544A9 1997
813′.54—dc20 96-34067
CIP

ISBN 0-385-48517-4

Printed in the United States of America

March 1997

First Edition

1 3 5 7 9 10 8 6 4 2

To
Shelley Jackson

1

I knew my way to Alice. I knew where to find her. I walked across campus that night writing a love plan in my head, a map across her body to follow later, when we were back in our apartment. It wouldn't be long. She was working late hours in the particle accelerator, studying minute bodies, pushing them together in collisions of unusual force and cataloging the results. I knew I'd find her there. I could see the swell of the cyclotron on the scrubby, sun-bleached hill as I walked the path to its tucked-away entrance. I was minutes away.

Unlike the physicists, my workday was over. My department couldn't pretend it was on the verge of something epochal. When the sun set we freed our graduate students to scatter to movie theaters, bowling alleys, pizza parlors. What hurry? We were studying local phenomena, recent affairs. The physicists were studying the beginning, so they rushed to describe or bring about the end.

As I hurtled toward her, carving shortcuts across the grass, violating the grid of concrete walkways, my heart was light. I was in orbit around Alice. I was a fizzy, spinning particle. I wanted to penetrate her field, see myself caught in her science gaze. Her Paradigm Eyes.

The supercollider stretched out, a lazy arm, across the piebald hills above campus. The old cyclotron was like a beehive on top. Underneath, a network of labs was dug into the hill. The complex grew, experiment by costly experiment, an architectural Frankenstein's Monster to crush the human spirit. But as I approached the entrance, double doors of scratched Plexiglas, I felt immune. I knew what lay at the heart of the heartless labyrinth. No immensity was enough to dwarf me.

So I stepped inside. The facility was made of bland slabs of concrete, as if to refute the hyperactive instability of the atomic world. The walls were run through at random with pipes and electric cables, painted gray to match the concrete. The floor thrummed slightly. The facility might have been a giant ventilation system, and I a speck or mote. But I had my target. I walked undaunted.

Alice's wing was empty, though. Alice was gone, and so were her students and colleagues. My footsteps echoing, I wandered the dingy concrete halls, searching the nearby labs. They were empty. Checked the muon-tank observation room. Empty. The computer center. I had never seen the computer center empty, without even a doleful supersymmetrist poring over high-resolution subatomic events, but it was empty now. I looked in at the beam-control room, but the doors were locked.

I was alone. Just me and the particles. I imagined them

resting at the end of a strenuous run through the supercollider, hovering in subzero silence, in states of calm nonexistence. The hum in my ears wasn't really the particles, of course, but it could have been my fear of them vibrating in me. I got out of there.

In the curve of the corridor I ran into another ghost, another human particle haunting the abandoned wing. A student, half in and half out of his sweatshirt, rushing to the exit. At the sound of my steps his head emerged from the neck of the shirt.

"Where is everybody?" I asked.

"It's Professor Soft," he said. "He's succeeded in opening up a Farhi-Guth Universe." He was so impatient to be past me that he burbled.

"Where?"

He pointed the way.

"Why are you leaving?"

"Soft wants footage, a document, to record the moment. I'm getting a camcorder. Reaction shots, in-camera editing."

"Good luck," I said.

He hurried away.

I went to the elevator. I knew about Soft's experiment, his bubble. It was the topic of plenty of hushed, reverent faculty discussions. I knew I should feel the breath of history at my neck as I plummeted down into the depths of the complex, to the laboratory where the false vacuum bubble was being reared under Soft's firm hand. Soft and his team were compressing matter, in an attempt to create a new universe.

The physics department, Alice included, specialized in the pursuit of tiny nothingness. Soft had the audacity to pursue a big nothingness. If his work succeeded the inflationary bubble would detach and grow into a universe tangential to ours. Another world. It would be impossible to detect, but equally real. Soft was merely trying to reproduce the big bang.

The crowd in the Cauchy-space lab observation room was oblivious to my arrival. Everyone was there: the students who ran the beam, the muon lab staff, the supersymmetrists, Alice and her students. They huddled in collective awe before the pixel-screen image of Soft's false vacuum bubble.

Soft stood with a wooden pointer aimed lazily at the radiant mass on the screen. His graduate student stood to one side of him. Soft's pride was concealed, but it gushed in proxy from his student. The crowd of upturned faces glowed with the light of the bright nothing on the screen.

"We had to devise a bubble geometry that featured spherical symmetry," explained Soft.

There was silence. We stared at the shimmering screen. They were pondering Soft's words. So was I, sort of.

"In order to adhere the Schwarzshild space to the De Sitter space," Soft continued, "we had to develop a pair of anti-trapped surfaces, in an asymptotically Minkowskian background."

A chorus of murmurs applauded the wisdom of this approach. Amen, I thought.

"The key was the quantum expectation value of the energy-momentum tensor."

I slipped unseen through the hypnotized crowd, to find Alice. She was gazing at the screen, her feet a little apart, her head back, her hair loose. I stepped up behind her and whispered her name (it was a whisper already, *Alice)* and put my arms around her. I fit my knees behind hers, her elbows inside mine, and cradled her folded arms, and inside them, her breasts.

"I can smell you," I said quietly.

5

She was distracted, a part of the bubble-event audience, not mine.

"I feel an initial singularity," I whispered. "Pressed against your spherical symmetry."

Nothing. She was deaf to me.

"I want to adhere my Schwarzshild space to your De Sitter space," I said.

No response.

"We'll make a little Schwarz-child."

Nothing.

Nothing. We stared up together, with all the others, at the wonderful nothing Soft had summoned up. The false vacuum region.

"Alice," I said.

"The bubble has to detach," Alice said, without taking her eyes away.

The student I'd met in the hallway returned with video equipment, and set up to record the great moment. I pictured handclasps, high fives, a roomful of physicists piled up like a victorious baseball team.

But not yet. The air of anticipation in the room was incredible. Alice, in my arms, was practically brittle with it. I felt my love plan slip away. I erased my evening's map across her body. Physics history came first. The false bubble had to detach.

It was there and then, in the dark heart of the physics complex, that I felt the first pangs of my coming loss.

My heart, to put it more simply, got nostalgic for the present. Always a bad sign.

The false vacuum bubble would not detach. At eleven-thirty the food service delivered bread, tuna fish, egg salad, milk, and wax paper, a midnight picnic in the clammy heart of the building. No one left. No one despaired of waiting. The false vacuum bubble wouldn't detach. The physicists milled in nervous clusters, expressing a solidarity that seemed feeble in that chilly core. At two the security guards delivered flimsy cots, pillows, woolly earthquake-victim blankets, fresh rolls of paper for the toilet stalls. No one slept.

The false bubble would not detach.

2

My dissertation work, five years earlier, was on "Theory as Neurosis in the Professional Scientist." On its strength I won an assistant professorship at the department of anthropology, University of North California at Beauchamp (pronounced *beach 'em)*. The September I arrived was the first time I'd been to California, apart from the job interview.

My attitude was terrible at first. I wasn't comfortable applying the social sciences, those fun-house mirrors, to real people engaged in real pursuits. It seemed presumptuous and unfair. So my tongue went into my cheek. My teaching suffered, and I was put through a severe departmental review.

Then I gained an insight, a purloined-letter kind of thing. The review itself was the key. I didn't have to look any further for my life's work. I would study academic environments, the departmental politics and territorial squabbles, the places where disciplines overlapped, fed back, and interfered. Like a parapsychologist, I set traps for the phantom curricula that wavered into existence in the void between actual ones. I applied information theory to the course catalogs, the reading lists, the food-service menus.

My new work was irrelevant and strong. It appeared only in translation, in the journal *Veroffentlichen Sonst Umkommen*, heavily footnoted articles, dry and unreadable as a handful of fine sand. My nickname around the department was the Dean of Interdiscipline. Interdean, for short. I got an apartment on campus, and there were days when I never crossed out of the benign square mile that included the buildings where I taught, ate dining-hall food, and read faculty notices on tattered, pinpricked bulletin boards.

It was some interdisciplinary project that first brought me to the gigantic and forbidding buildings that were the physics department, and got me grappling with the gigantic and forbidding theories that were modern physics. Even for the Interdean, that stuff was rough going. My reward was that hidden inside the theories and buildings, like a pearl in an oyster, was the new assistant professor specializing in particle physics, Alice Coombs.

I kept cooking up stupid questions, excuses to visit the collider where Alice was running her particles like champion greyhounds. It was a few weeks before I had the courage to ask her out. I suggested a walk in the hills that overlooked the cyclotron. I think it was my first time off campus in a month. I remember Alice with her hands in the pockets of her lab coat, picking her way over exposed roots in the path. The sky was some dramatic uptilted cloudscape. Like the clouds were escaping to the stars. Beauchamp beneath us, toy city. I remember thinking, I don't like blond hair. But I liked Alice's. I was an idiot. Out of breath from climbing, we stumbled into each other on the path and I smelled her. If olives were sweet—that was how she smelled.

"It's funny like—"

"You reminded me—"

"We're hardly—"

Talk was hopeless. We smiled apologetically, while our words went spilling like platefuls of barbecue sauce onto a white dress in a detergent ad, comical slow-motion disaster.

I could only kiss her. That worked. I got another whiff of the sweetness of olives.

Alice Coombs and I soon learned to do many things together, including talk. We could even banter. Argue, if necessary. But we maintained a little cult of leaving things unsaid. Somehow we were wiser with our mouths shut, knew each other better.

Or so we thought.

The silence is where the idea of asking Alice to marry me got lost, stranded forever on the tip of my tongue. It was too obvious and uncouth. Too institutional. We'd been living together for nearly a year now, anthropology and physics. I cooked dinner most nights. Alice worked late.

3

I woke in the grip of a terrifying dream, involving tribesmen, clouds of dust, my answering machine. I was actually on a cot in the curved hallway outside the Cauchy-space lab. Alone. Finding myself in the bowels of the chilly, humming complex was stranger than the dream, and worse. It was like I'd been sleeping in the safe of a sunken ocean liner.

I'd fallen asleep at four in the morning. Professor Soft's inflationary universe had still been perversely refusing to perform. The bubble wouldn't detach. I'd gotten bored waiting and climbed onto one of the cots. Now I heard Alice's voice inside the observation room.

I went inside. The floor of the lab was littered with wax paper, empty pint containers, and crumpled printouts. The physicists had mostly curled on cots, or slumped home. Only a few remained, sore-eyed, waiting. Soft was scribbling notes at his portable workbench. His graduate student was still at his side.

11

The pixels oscillated serenely overhead. Alice stood where I'd left her. How long had I slept?

I took her hand. "What time is it?" I whispered.

"Out here it's eight-thirty," she said. "Inside the Cauchy-space it's still six yesterday. Time collapsed around the bubble event."

"Did it happen?"

"The wormhole dilated," she said.

"That's good."

Alice shook her head, still watching the screen. "It sounds good, but it isn't actually good. The bubble may actually have detached, as planned. But there shouldn't be an aneurysm."

"A wound?" I said.

"A hole."

"What does it mean?"

Alice shook her head.

"Is Soft very upset?"

"Look at his student."

I looked. It was true. Soft was a pillar of strength, but his graduate student was a mess, hair matted with nervous sweat, eyes shrunken from weeping. I looked up at the screen, and tried to make out the aneurysm. I couldn't see anything. The physicist in me was a blind, stunted thing.

I held Alice's cool hand and watched her watching the screen. She still couldn't spare a look to meet my eyes, couldn't tear herself from the impossibly boring experiment.

"Alice." I squeezed her hand.

She turned and kissed me. A small, measured kiss that landed on the edge of my mouth.

I put my thumbs under her eyes, where the flesh was gray and tender, and kissed her again.

12

"You have a class," she said.

"There's time to have breakfast."

She looked up at the screen, then down at the floor. I could tell she didn't want to talk here. "I have to stay," she said.

"This is important?"

"Very."

I smiled, but I wasn't happy. I wanted *Philip* to be playing on her screen now.

In the corner several physicists had gathered at Soft's desk, drinking at his murmured explanations like animals at a desert hole. Alice saw me looking and turned. She obviously wanted to join them.

I put my hands in her hair, and gently tilted her head to mine.

"I'll call you after your class," she whispered.

"Okay."

"I do want to see you."

"I know."

"I have to see this through. It's how I am. I like to be on the edge of the territory."

"The horizon of the real," I whispered.

Alice and I were the same size. We displaced the same amount of air. But when we embraced she became elusive and darting, like a remora fish. When I held her I imagined that I could crane my neck and kiss the small of her back, or reach around to clasp my own shoulders in my hands.

"Okay," I said. "Call me after class."

"You'll be at the apartment?"

I nodded. "I'll be defrosting something."

"I'll call you."

"With a bubble update. I'm genuinely interested."

13

We detached. She joined the confluence at Soft's desk. I felt a rustle of jealousy, but couldn't fix it to a target. It blurred and vanished.

As I came up out of the gray, timeless physics facility, into the nine o'clock light of campus, my heart lightened. I should have been exhausted, but I felt like a butterfly emerging from a cocoon. I had an edge on the bleary students on the grass-fringed paths. I alone knew of the aneurysm, the puckered bubble that lurked below. Here windows in white clapboard buildings squeaked open to admit the light, here the groundsmen plucked rubbish off the vast, waking lawns, here freshmen blinked away Zima hangovers. For them another day, but I knew time had stopped in its place.

A new universe. I pictured it twisting away from this one, kicking free of the umbilical wormhole in Soft's lab. The notion shed an odd, fresh light on the morning, on the twittering birds overhead, the chalk-slash of cloud, the student-council election flyers taped everywhere. Maybe this was the new universe, and Soft's monster had sucked away all staleness to the far ends of the galaxy.

Vowing to impart some hint of this vision in my lecture, I skipped toward the cafeteria, for a breakfast of Team, or Total.

4

The phone in our apartment was portable, and it was too nice a day to sit and wait for it to ring indoors. I set it out on the patio. I brought along iced tea and a book I knew I didn't want to read. But as soon as I sat down I heard voices, odd voices, at the front of the building.

"We've been here before," said the first voice.

"This is the place," said the second.

"We're three blocks from the pay phone," said the first.

"Correction," said the second. "Four blocks from the bus stop."

"The pay phone and the bus stop are two blocks apart."

"I think we're speaking of two different pay phones."

"There's only one pay phone. I mean, we only speak of one pay phone."

"Correction. Today is Tuesday. On Tuesday evenings we

see Cynthia Jalter. We change buses. The second pay phone is two blocks from the *transfer point.* On Tuesday there are two pay phones."

"You mean on Tuesday we speak of two pay phones."

"Right. Today is Tuesday. We are currently three blocks from the pay phone and five blocks from the pay phone. What time is it?"

There was a long pause.

"Four-thirty-seven," said the second voice. "Check your watch."

"Four-thirty-seven," said the first.

"Good. We're on time. This is the place."

"Yes, we've been here before. Shall we ring the bell?"

"Do you want to do it?"

"All right."

Again, a long silence. Finally, the doorbell. I stayed put. I couldn't imagine that these comedians had any real business on our doorstep.

"No answer," said the second voice.

"Are we late?"

A pause. "It's four-thirty-eight. This is the right time. Is it the right place?"

"It's the right place. We've been here before. We walked from the bus stop."

"Where is Miss Coombs?"

"Correction. Professor Coombs."

"Is she late?"

"We might be early. What time is it?"

Now I got out of my deck chair. I wanted to break the loop of their talk, save all three of us from going through any more of it.

16

"Hello," I said, as I rounded the corner of the building. Then, seeing them, I stopped and shut up. At the door stood two blind men, one black, one white, both in wrinkled black two-piece suits, both with canes. They turned their heads as I arrived, not to face me with their useless eyes, but to cock their ears, like German shepherds.

The blindness explained the lag reading watches and ringing doorbells, and some of the oddness of their talk.

"Hello," answered the black man, who'd been the first voice. "Could you tell us if this is where Professor Coombs resides?"

I had them wait inside while I collected the telephone from the patio. Our apartment was simple enough: two bedrooms off a central kitchen and living room, divided by a counter. They inhabited it like oversize windup toys, scuttling into corners and rebounding to meet in the middle, canes dueling. They ran their hands everywhere, mapping frantically, too frantically. I eventually had to lead them each to the couch, though they'd both touched it more than once in their survey.

"We're roommates," explained the white man, the second voice. "I'm Evan Robart."

"Philip Engstrand," I said, and took his hand.

"Garth Poys," said the other. I tugged free of one handshake and entered another.

"Alice should be back soon," I said. "Can I offer either of you a drink?"

"No," said Evan Robart. "I had something to drink before I left the house."

"We both did," said Garth Poys.

"We're here to talk to Professor Coombs about an experiment," Evan said. "It involves Garth."

17

"I apparently possess blindsight," said Garth. "Not that it's doing me much good." He delivered this like the punchline of a joke he didn't find particularly funny.

"Miss Coombs apparently feels this qualifies him as a physicist," said Evan. He spoke in the same ironic, world-weary tone.

"Correction. Professor Coombs. Huh."

I sat, dumbfounded by the ping-pong clatter of their talk. I was doing my best to look comfortable, my mouth clenched in a smile, my legs crossed, all the while failing to produce the one signal that might be received—speech.

"Do you have the time?"

"Quarter to five," I squeaked.

"Really? I've got four-forty-two. Evan?"

"Same. At least we're synchronized. That's something."

"Do you think I'm right?" Garth asked me. "Who do you think is wrong?"

"I'm probably wrong," I managed.

Garth turned his head toward Evan. His eyes were open a little, slits of white beneath his near-purple lids, twin moons smiling in the night of his face. "We could all be wrong," he said gravely.

There was a sound at the door. Alice came in, arms loaded with straining bags of groceries, celery and paper towels poking out at the top. She peered over the top and offered superfluous introductions as she juggled the bags into the kitchen.

I followed her in and cleared space on the counter, which was crammed with humming, ready appliances. We unpacked. Alice sorted out dinner. Green peas, salmon, rice, avocado, ice cream. The rest we crammed into cupboards. I waited for the sound of running water to cover my voice.

"They're incredible."

18

"They can't help it."

"The talk. It's obsessive."

"Compensation. They can't see. They map their environment verbally."

"It requires a lot of confirmation, this map."

"Listen to them. It's poetic."

"Synchronizing their watches constantly. Like astronauts."

Alice put on water for rice, rinsed the peas, skinned the avocado. I offered the blind men drinks again. They refused again. We listened as they quietly and persistently mapped the living room, negotiating over the distances between various landmarks, the floor lamp, the fireplace, the doorstep. I cut a lemon.

"What about the aneurysm? What happened?"

"The breach stabilized."

"Breach?"

"Soft upgraded it to breach status."

"Worse or better than aneurysm?"

"Different. More stable."

"But completely unexpected."

"In retrospect less so. I took it to my computer this afternoon. My equations don't balance unless I allow for the portal."

"Portal or breach? There seems to be some blurriness."

"Soft calls it a breach," she said. "I call it a portal."

"It's Soft's thing."

"If I describe it it's my thing. I'm getting interested." She was turned away from me, slicing avocado, crushing herbs. Inside I heard the blind men talking of bus stops and pay phones.

"I thought you already were interested."

"When it was going to detach it was more Soft's kind of thing," she said. "But it's still here. That's my kind of thing."

19

"You like perceptible things," I suggested. "You like to make measurements."

"Not easily perceptible," she pointed out. "Just barely present."

"It's all colors," I said.

"What?"

"The food. You're cooking for blind men, and it's all colors. Green peas, blueberry ice cream, salmon. Avocado."

We stared at each other.

"Will they feel like they're missing something?" she whispered.

"It must happen sometimes. I mean, they *are* missing something."

We took dinner out and set the table hastily around it. The blind men, led to the table, became formal and quiet. I could see them browsing the collage of smells and sounds, the gentle clinking of silverware and ice. Alice filled the plates, and we ate, the blind men leaning over their plates, forking up unknown quantities to meet trembling lips. Peas and rice tumbled back to the table.

Alice began to talk. "In physics we have an observer problem," she said. "Suppose we take a spinning electron and observe which direction its spin axis lies along. We find, oddly enough, that it lies along whatever direction we choose to observe from."

"An observer problem, huh," said Garth, with disturbing emphasis.

"This chicken is very good," said Evan.

"We rarely have chicken," said Garth.

We were eating fish. I said nothing.

20

"Some people think the observer's consciousness determines the spin or even the existence of the electron."

"I believe the salt is three, maybe four inches to the right of your plate."

"More like five."

"That's probably closer to my plate, then."

"It's a problem of subjectivity, really. How can the observer make an objective observation? It's impossible."

"A problem of subjectivity. Huh."

I wanted to interrupt. Alice's effort seemed hopeless. I hadn't learned yet that Evan and Garth were listening.

"We spoke about this before, didn't we?" said Garth. "In her office, last Friday."

"Yes, that's right," said Evan. A grain of rice clung to his upper lip. "In her office."

"About what time?"

"About three in the afternoon."

"Roughly ninety-six hours ago. Is that what you're saying?"

"That's about right."

"Huh." Garth raised his head, aimed his eyes at the ceiling. Alice and I looked at him.

"Well," he said, "we got a book."

"From the library," said Evan.

"We read about it. The observer problem."

"That's wonderful," said Alice.

"She says it's wonderful," said Evan, as if Garth couldn't hear anyone but him.

"I think I understand," said Garth. "It's a problem of subjectivity, knowing. Thinking. Observing is like thinking."

"Yes."

21

"Except for me. I can see without thinking. That's what they mean by blindsight. Not that it's doing me any good. Huh."

"Yes," said Alice again. The white man and the black man smiled. Some kind of understanding had been reached. I was alone in my confusion.

"What's blindsight?" I said.

"He wants to know what blindsight is." They snorted over private ironies. "Do you want to tell him?"

"I'll tell him. What time is it?"

"Five-fifty-seven. What time is the last bus?"

"Eleven. I've got five-fifty-eight."

They reset and corroborated the bulky braille watches. Garth leaned back in his chair and fixed his ungaze on a point a foot or so to the left of my face. "Evan and I are blind in different ways," he said. "Evan has eyes that don't work. There's nothing wrong with my eyes."

"I'm amaurotic," said Evan, with a hint of pride.

"My eyes work fine," said Garth. "But I have an atrophy of a part of my brain associated with visual awareness." He was quoting some text, I could tell. "My eyes work fine. I can see. I just don't know I can see."

"He can't know."

"My brain doesn't understand sight."

"Blindsight," said Alice excitedly, "is when you trick Garth into forgetting he doesn't know he can see. The doctor commands him to reach for an object. He grabs it without hesitation. When the doctors trace the vectors of his hands, arms, fingers, and the movement of his eyes, they're all precise. He still doesn't experience sight, but he's unquestionably seeing. Making an observation."

"Not that it does me any good. Huh."

It slowly sank in. "Observation without consciousness," I said.

"Observation without subjective judgment," said Alice.

"The spin of a particle," I said.

"Physics," said Alice.

"Your office is in the physics building," said Evan.

"We were there," said Garth. "It's about five blocks from the bus stop."

5

Alice and I had sex that night. For a long time afterward we didn't talk. The bedroom was dark and cool. Light leaked in from the hall and outlined our bodies in the darkness as we lay still, sweating where we overlapped, goose-pimpled where we didn't. The quiet was rich with things unsaid.

We didn't speak of Soft's experiment, the breach or portal. We didn't mention the blind men, or Alice's dream of a perfect, sightless physicist.

Soon Alice was falling asleep, and I wasn't. I heard the air flutter between her lips.

"Alice."

"Philip?"

"Where do I stop and you begin?"

She hesitated. "You mean what is the cut-off point?"

"I mean if you went away what would be left of me?"

"I'm not going away." Her voice was very quiet.

"But answer anyway."

"All of you would be left," she said. "None of me. I would be gone and you would still be here."

I could tell she wanted to sleep. But it was as though letting her sleep tonight was the same as losing her.

"You complete me," I said. "I'm not sure I really exist, except under your observation."

She didn't say anything.

"If you left me," I said, "you'd take so much of me with you that I'd be inside you, looking back at what was left—the husk of Philip Engstrand we'd abandoned."

She stared at me across the pillow. "That's actually beautiful," she said.

"So when I feel distance between us it's like there's something wrong between me and myself. I feel a gulf in myself."

Alice closed her eyes. "Nothing's wrong," she said.

"No?" I said.

"I was up all night. I have to sleep. That's all."

"Okay," I said. "I just—"

"Philip, stop, please."

I held her while she cried. When her body stopped trembling, she was asleep.

Days passed. Classes were taught, seminars held. Papers were handed in, graded, and returned. The team won something, and the trees filled with garlands of toilet paper. It rained, and the toilet paper dripped to the pathways, and into the wiper blades of parked cars. A group of students seized the Frank J. Bellhope Memorial Aquarium to protest the treatment of Roberta, the manatee savant. The protest was a failure. I called a symposium on the history of student seizure of campus buildings. The symposium was a success. In the larger world, the team invaded something, some hapless island or isthmus. A letter of protest by the faculty was drafted, revised, and scrapped. Bins of swollen pumpkins appeared in the produce sections of Fastway and Look 'n' Like.

Alice went on demolishing particles. When I saw her she was distracted, absent. She worked long days with her graduate students and with Garth Poys, Blind Physicist, readying a series of proton runs. Nights she spent huddled with Soft in the Cauchy-space observation room, following the progress of the breach or portal. I sometimes brought sandwiches to her in the long chilly arm of the accelerator, but I drew a line at descending again into that dark heart where Soft's monster lurked.

I first heard the name *Lack* in the campus barbershop. The barbers there specialized in crew cuts and baldings for the campus athletes, the swimmers, wrestlers, and football players. The walls were layered with programs and posters, autographed by college stars long since graduated into painful, grinding NFL careers. When I strolled in, maybe six times a year, my barber would sigh, put down his electric clipper, and search out the misplaced thinning shears.

Today Soft was sitting in the waiting area, his hands folded primly. I hardly recognized him without his lab coat and pointer, his Nobel aura. He was a pale underground thing wandering in the upper world. It was a shock that his hair grew.

"Soft," I said.

"Engstrand."

"The breach is untended," I said playfully. "You've left it."

"Students are there around the clock," he said.

"What if something happens?"

"Nothing will happen. The lack is stabilized."

"The lack?"

"We're calling it that." He sounded a little uncomfortable.

"So it's stopped being an 'event,' " I said. "Now it's defined by it's failure to 'happen.' An absence, a lack."

"We're no longer defining it as a failure. Just a lack."

"Gentlemen."

"He was first," I pointed out.

27

"We can take you both."

Soft and I climbed into adjoining chairs, and were cranked into position. The long mirror framed us together, sitting passively with white bibs tucked up around our collars. The bottom edge of this picture was littered with gels, combs, and sprays.

"Style or trim?"

"Short back and sides."

"Trim, just around the neck and ears. You mean to say it's not a breach anymore?"

"Breach was a misdefinition. There was a lack all along. It was initially accompanied by a gravity event, which in turn resulted in a time event."

"Not too much off the top. But it's not accompanied by a gravity event now?"

"It's no longer accompanied by any type of event. It's entirely clean."

"Lean forward."

"Clean how?"

"There's nothing but the lack."

"Nothing but the lack," I repeated. "How do you know you've got the lack, then?"

"Particle counts, particles that should be there but aren't. A trace imbalance in the M's and H's in the lab."

"God, that's short. You mean it's eating particles?"

"Mr. Engstrand, in a week you'll thank me."

"In layman's terms, eating them, yes. They drift toward the lack and fail to appear on the other side."

"What does it mean?"

"We're at a point of theorizing wildly. For example, Alice and I disagree."

"What's your theory?"

28

"I'm glad you asked. It's my opinion that the creation event is being infinitely reproduced. The missing particles are fueling continuous inflation. The lack is the hub."

"You mean it's reproducing the original experiment? The universe-in-a-lab?"

"Yes."

"So it's just spinning out universes, one after another?"

"Yes. But that's just my opinion."

"Alice?"

"Ask her yourself."

"Here, have a look at the back."

The barber handed me a mirror and turned my chair around, and for a moment I was trapped in a world of infinite regress, a never-ending reflective corridor of Engstrands, Softs, barbers, gels, and too-short haircuts. I nodded my approval and handed the mirror back.

Soft and I went out together. I ran my fingers through my hair to make it stand up, he carefully patted his to make it lie flat. We crossed the street in a crowd of murmuring, gossiping students, back onto campus. The day was glorious and the air was choked with Frisbees, the lawn strewn with slighted textbooks.

"Soft, Lord of Universes," I said.

"I only meant to create one. And I could be wrong."

"Endless Soft Universes, the lack twitching them out like origami cranes."

"I imagine I'm probably completely wrong."

I was liking the way it defied theory, the way it had the physicists scrambling. Breach, gap, gulf, hub—the lack was obviously an explosion of metaphor into a literal world. I felt a secret kinship with it.

29

Then Soft, ever so casually and indifferently, broke my heart.

"Alice is a curious case," he said. "She's in a very awkward position. I envy you."

"Sorry?"

"I mean, she has an incredible subjectivity problem. If she were a bit less in love she might do less crappy physics, but we wouldn't want that, would we?"

"Well—"

"I've watched her do a lot of physics in the last few weeks. I've had a lot of opportunities. She's mistaken the gloriously random mechanism that is the universe for a locket, in a manner of speaking."

"What are you saying?"

"It's a commonplace among physicists, Philip, that when one of our rank succumbs to mysticism it's because of passion. Something projected out of the physicist's private life, into the experiment. That's what I see in Alice. She's completely without the proper outlook. You must be a very happy man."

"Uh, yes."

He seemed pleased. We'd stopped on the commons' lawn, where clusters of students lay prone in the sun.

"I'm glad we had this chance," he said.

"Yes."

He tittered. "Don't go around speaking of Soft Universes."

"Yes. No. Don't worry."

He walked away in his bad new haircut, looking for the entrance to his burrow, I guess. I stood rooted to the lawn. I felt stiff but bent, off-center, like a plank warped by storage in a mildewy cellar.

Soft had described an Alice I didn't recognize, an Alice

who was different from mine. The Alice I knew was obsessed with objectivity. She'd never permitted her heart a voice in her work. What's more, I'd never seen her less in love, less swayed by passion. These last few weeks she'd lived in the physics facility, not our apartment. No, Soft's Alice wasn't the same as mine.

Except she had to be, of course. They were one and the same.

So the passion he'd seen in her wasn't for me.

7

Could Alice love a blind man? Evan. Of the two of them, Evan seemed less inflexible. His part in the verbal remapping was wifely, supportive. Garth was the obsessor. And Evan had a certain skewed charisma, a Buster Keaton charm in his wrinkled suit. One-way gazes were infatuations, crushes. In that way a blind man was like an actor or rock star. Had Alice lost herself peering into the void of his eyes? I'm amaurotic, he'd said. I'm erotic. I pictured Alice folding his suit into a neat pile on a chair, kissing trembling, half-closed lids, guiding blind hands to her breasts. Nipples hard like braille.

Or Garth. Garth was her star, her Blind Physicist. But he struck me as a borderline autistic. Together with Evan he formed a closed system as perfect and impervious as a perpetual-motion device. I couldn't imagine Garth without Evan.

Evan and Garth, then. A nightmare of Alice lost in the

tangle of groping, clumsy limbs. Their mapping and remapping of the surface of her body, coordinating distances between landmarks and entrances.

What about Soft himself? Could Alice love that pasty, underground creature? Remotely possible. There was his greatness, his Prize. I pictured long nights in the Cauchy-space lab. Lonely discoveries, unexpected parities, one hand reaching to still the trembling of another as it jotted down formulae.

But then why would Soft talk to me about her passion? Couldn't he see that he was the reason her physics had gotten "crappy"? So he was taunting me, toying with me. A classic example of a physicist's contempt for other disciplines. I balled my fists.

What if it was somebody else, though? Another faculty member, from the English department. A decoder of sonnets. His sentences finer than mine, metaphors less grotesquely modern. Or a student, a graduate student in physics. Soft's maybe, stepping out from behind his mentor, becoming real.

Somebody else. Somebody other. Some other body.

Alice with Mr. Someotherbody.

8

My heart and the elevator, a plummet inside a plummet. Down into my stomach and the gloomy core of the physics complex, to walk those barren concrete corridors, brave those sterile labs, in search of what I'd lost. Where else could I go? I'd phoned in cancellation of my afternoon thesis tutorial, then wandered campus, hesitating like a ghost at mailboxes, bulletin boards, and coffee machines, but there was no pretending. I was looking for Alice.

I stepped out of the elevator into a parade of students wearing radiation suits. They were carrying delicate chunks of electronic equipment through the Cauchy-space lab. Something important was happening, I thought bitterly. They were back on the verge of making history.

Unnoticed, I went inside. The observation room was filling with dismantled electronics, set onto cushioned pallets and draped with anti-static drop cloths. The screen overhead was black. The student technicians padded in and out in their white clown suits, headset radios buzzing and clicking. Robots, but they had more in common with Alice than I did. They were the same species. Physicists. I was some other thing, a spider or rabbit or carrot.

A student in a lab coat stopped in front of me. I recognized him. Part of Alice's inner circle.

"Mr. Engstrand."

"Yes."

"You want to talk to Ms. Coombs?"

"Yes."

"Follow me."

He gave me a suit and hood, helped me seal myself inside, and pointed out the buttons that operated the headset radio, the private frequency that would link me to Alice. Before I could object he aimed me through the airlock doors, into the outer chamber of the Cauchy-space lab. The doors opened and sealed behind me automatically as I stumbled through, no physicist, just a clumsy earthbound astronaut, a beekeeper.

The outer chamber was a narrow, dimly lit area, separated from the Cauchy-space by a thickness of Plexiglas. I was alone there. White-suited figures ambled about on the other side of the glass, in the garishly floodlit lab, like spirits trapped in a bottle. They were dismantling the equipment that lined the walls, winding cables, decompressing valves, gathering washers and fittings in their soft white gloves. I was invisible at my dark window. I could only guess which was Alice.

The lack is gone, I thought hopefully. It's all over. They're mopping up.

I pushed the button and spoke into the headset mouthpiece. "Alice." My own voice was piped back to my ear, rendered mechanical and feeble, a toaster or vacuum cleaner bidding for human attention. But one of the figures turned to face me at my window.

As the mask of its hood passed through the light I saw it was Alice. She unclipped a lamp and brought it to shine through the window. When she leaned her headgear against her side of the glass the reflections were layered, so my features were superimposed over hers.

"Philip," she said, through static.

"What are you doing?"

"Lack is ready. We're taking down the field."

"Lack?"

"He's stabilized. We don't need to maintain the Cauchy-field anymore. Gravity and time are compatible. We're dismantling the generators."

"Soft says 'the lack,' and 'it.' Not 'Lack' and 'he.' "

"Soft and I disagree."

"Soft says your physics are crappy. He says you don't have the right outlook."

"Soft is retrenching. It's his physics that are crappy. He refuses to admit that Lack has a preference for H's."

"What?"

"Lack is selective. He prefers H's. M's pass through him and accumulate on the screen. So he's making selections. It's not random. It's discernment, intelligence."

I fell silent. Our channel buzzed.

"Soft is predisposed against void intelligence," said Alice. "It threatens him."

"You're saying Lack displays intelligence?"

"Lack *is* intelligence, Philip. There's nothing else there. He has no other qualities. Without gravity and time irregularities he's impossible to measure. His only aspect is his preference for the H's."

"So far."

"You're right, I think there's more. In a few days we'll be able to walk through this chamber in our street clothes."

"Then what?"

"We'll be able to bring subtler instruments to bear."

"Tarot cards, you mean. Magic eight-balls. Seeing-eye dogs."

Alice frowned through three layers of glass. I realized I had no stake in siding with Soft. I hadn't come here to debate "Lack's" nature.

"Alice," I said again. I winced at the electronic slush the radio made of my whisper.

She didn't speak.

"Alice, let's quit. Let's go away." I knew it was wrong as I said it. I was breaking the silence that bound us. I might as well ask her to marry me now.

"What?"

"Let's disappear together. Leave no gravity or time irregularities behind."

"This isn't the right time to suggest that."

"That's what's great about it," I said. "It wouldn't be exciting if there was a right time."

I was testing her. It was better than blurting out accusations, at least a little.

Another voice came onto the channel, encrusted with static. "Excuse me, Ms. Coombs."

"That's all right."

"We're ready to distribute the yeast."

37

"I'll be there in a minute."

The voice crackled away.

"Yeast?" I said.

"G. P. Neumann Yeast. It was developed by a German firm for use in reactor settings. It devours radiation. We're using it to clean the chamber."

I didn't know what to say. My momentum was gone. I was in a floppy suit discussing yeast.

"Philip?"

I looked up. She'd stepped back behind the lamp, so her own face-place was reflective. I saw two of myself, and none of her.

"We'll talk later, okay, Philip?"

"Okay." I wanted to say no, later isn't soon enough. A German yeast is about to devour the radioactive traces of my hands on your body, the isotope emanations of my heart. They're delicate things, no match for yeast.

But I didn't say it. I plodded back through the airlock and waited to be helped out of my suit, like a child in clip-on mittens standing in a puddle of melted snow.

A student with a clipboard was checking off items in a Buddhist monotone. "Gas barriers. Scintillation counters. Photomultipliers. Photodiodes, phototriodes."

I left the lab.

In the corridor I found myself on the heels of Alice's blind men. They were tapping with their canes to the elevator. I slowed and stayed behind them, wary, jealous, not wanting to be detected.

They hesitated at the sound of my footsteps, then shrugged together and groped at the elevator doorway for the button.

"You must have done something wrong," said Evan.

Garth didn't speak.

"You must have done something wrong," said Evan again.

Nothing.

"You must have done something wrong."

"What time is it?" said Garth. They groped their watches.

"Two-fifty-seven."

"Right. At least we're synchronized. I didn't do anything wrong. I saw a particle."

"I don't think you did it right."

"She wanted to measure the spin. But there wasn't any spin. It wasn't spinning. Huh."

"That was no particle."

The elevator doors opened. They stepped inside, and I followed. They bustled into the rear, canes tangling.

"Would you press *lobby?*" said Evan.

I hit the button.

"Whoever it is, they're probably going to the lobby too, you know," said Garth, as if I couldn't hear it.

"We can't be sure," said Evan.

"Probably about seventy-five percent of the people in a given elevator are going to the lobby," said Garth.

"Unless they got on at the lobby," said Evan.

I remained silent.

"You didn't see anything," said Evan, a little viciously. "That's why she has no use for you. That wasn't a particle."

"How would you know?"

"It wasn't a particle. It wasn't anything."

"Correction. I don't see things that aren't there. That's the whole point."

The elevator opened to the lobby and I stepped out.

"Lobby?" said Evan.

39

I didn't speak.

"It sounds like the lobby," said Garth.

"We're about five blocks from the bus stop," said Evan as they came out of the elevator.

"We should be there in about five minutes."

"It took four minutes on the way over. Not that there was any reason to rush, as things turned out."

They tapped past me, toward the breeze and its smells, the chirping insects, the warm invisible sunlight. The bus stops and parking meters waiting to be cataloged and curated.

My mystery had deepened. The blind men were like me and Soft. They stood outside of Alice's narrowing circle of favor. I'd have to find other suspects.

Garth paused at the entrance and raised his head, wrinkling his nose as though detecting my presence by scent. He pursed his lips and frowned, like a bullfrog. "At least I saw a particle," he said, as much in my direction as Evan's. "She never had any use for you in the first place."

Alice never packed a bag. Her time in the apartment just dwindled. I pretended we were suffering a temporary rift, and that in her silent way she would slip back into my arms. Four or five lonely nights had passed before the morning I cornered her in the hall of the administration building.

"Philip," she said, almost sweetly.

"Alice."

"I have to stay with Lack," she said. "He can't be left unobserved."

Neither can I, I wanted to say.

"I'm canceling my classes. This is a big opportunity. Lack's all mine now. I understand what he's saying. I'm the only one."

"You're the only one for Lack."

"Yes."

It was work holding back my sarcasm. The result was silence.

10

When Alice held her press conference I crept in and sat unobtrusively at the back. It turned out that Alice was right, Soft wrong. Lack was displaying a preference for certain particles. There wasn't any explanation, but Alice had dubbed it *vacuum intelligence,* and Lack was instantly and forever anthropomorphized.

Lack had star potential, at least on campus. He was a charismatic mystery, a mute ambassador, a cosmic Kaspar Hauser. Developments in his chamber went murmuring through the faculty daily. And today he was being offered to the larger world.

The larger world was showing only the slightest interest. The conference hall was less than half full, and I recognized a lot of the faces. The physicists might have overestimated Lack's sex appeal. Alice sat up on the dais, sipping water and paging through her notes, unperturbable, wrapped in silence. Soft was

41

"Philip. You understand, don't you?"

I closed my eyes, leaned against the wall. "You're sleeping with Lack."

She ignored the provocation. "I'm sleeping in the lab. I mean, I'm not really sleeping much, to tell the truth. Please understand, Philip. I'm on the edge of the territory."

Horizon of the real, I silently corrected.

A desultory student passed us in the hall, headed for some office to beg for reprieve.

"You're leaving me," I said.

"I have to be where this takes me."

"It takes you away. You're gone, and I'm alone."

"You're not alone."

"Worse than alone, actually. I'm partial. I'm part of something that isn't there anymore. I'm a broken-off chunk."

Alice looked down. "What I'm doing is very important."

"When will you come back?"

Silence.

"Say something encouraging," I said. "Tell me it's good for us. Tell me you think I'm overreacting. Use the word *us.*"

She met my eyes with a look of terror.

"What I'm hearing is you won't use the word *us,*" I said.

She stared at her feet again. "Soft once told me that certain discoveries choose the scientist who discovers them. They wait for the right one. That's me and Lack."

Welling sarcasm again drowned my tongue.

Alice took my hand. "I have to go, Philip."

"To Lack."

"Yes." She pulled her hand away, ran hair out of her eyes, smiled feebly. "I'm sorry."

Before I could speak she was gone.

beside her, his legs crossed, pants hitched up awkwardly to reveal spindly ankles, his expression distant. The momentum in the department belonged to Alice now. Soft was just a token, a reminder of the Prize that could be had.

The lights dimmed. Alice stepped up to the podium, waiting for the crowd to fall silent, and introduced herself and Soft. Then she explained, in lucid detail, the sequence that had led to the discovery and naming of Lack. Soft's venture, the false vacuum bubble. The aneurysm. The gravity event. The audience followed her closely.

My attention wandered. I was busy righting myself. It was useful, seeing Alice at a fixed distance, so far away. She was up there, and I was over here, she was apparently intact—maybe I was intact, too. So I sat and adjusted my own vertical hold after a week of spinning.

Alice went on to describe the state of the experiment—Lack's gradual stabilization, and the conversion of the chamber from Cauchy-space to earth-normal. "Lack's tastes make up his being," she said. "His preference for certain particles is all there is to him. If he stops choosing he stops existing." She described the attempt to define his exact boundaries, the array of detectors, meters, and photosensitive plates they had aimed at this hint, this tenuous invisible presence.

The audience applauded politely when she was done. Alice nodded her thanks and went to sit beside Soft, to field questions from the crowd.

The questions that came were respectful and daunted. I lost my patience with the whole thing. I suddenly wanted to be out in the world. The campus, that is. But when I got to my feet I was mistaken for a questioner.

44

"Yes? Professor Engstrand?" said Alice. Her amplified voice boomed in the auditorium. A student with a microphone hurried toward me through the crowd, trailing cord.

It was a silly mistake. I'd been feeling invisible, but I was a recognizable figure. The Interdean should have something to say about Lack.

I hated to disappoint. So I took the microphone. As I weighed it in my hand I felt the spotlight of the crowd's attention swing toward me, heard it in the creaking of chairs.

"It's a conceit of physics," I said, "that the rest of the world exists to supply metaphors for subatomic events. The *spin* of a particle, the *color* or *flavor* of a quark. A *field* or *horizon*. *Beauty*, *truth*, and *strangeness*. The physicist tends to see his subject as the indivisible core around which metaphor orbits. Physics is the universal tongue, the language the aliens will speak when they appear."

Some instinct led me to pause. I let the microphone drop to my waist. The audience looked up at Alice and Soft, searching their faces for response.

I am the Lorax, I thought. I speak for the trees.

"I have to question the assumption that Lack's preference is for particles, in and of themselves," I continued. "Why do we assume that our visitor is a physicist, that he finds particles interesting? So he prefers H's to M's. What about summer and winter? Which does he like best? Black and white, or color? Poetry or prose? Bebop or swing? I think we're leading the witness. Our questions are dictating his answers. We want physics, so we get physics. But until we ask every question we can think to ask we're—pardon me—failing to do anything except masturbate in front of a mirror."

My grand statement. If only I could reel it back in, swallow it, dissolve it in the acids of my stomach. For that's when I played my part, with Soft and Alice, in our collective Dr. Frankenstein. That was how I conspired in the creation of my own monstrous rival, my personal Stanley Toothbrush.

Would it have occurred without my help? I'll never know. But until then I'd been passive, a victim of fate. Now I was as much to blame as anyone.

11

The next day the microactivity detectors were dismantled, and the proton gun wheeled away. In their place a small lab table was rolled up to the bottom edge of Lack's particle strike zone. Otherwise Lack was left bare. Alice cleared the room of observers, locked the outer doors, and began the experiments that would etch her name forever in the history of physics.

The first was a paper clip, I think. Just a curled steel wire. She slid it across the table, pulling her hand away just short of the calibration that indicated Lack's edge. The paper clip slid across the table, through Lack, and dropped to the floor on the other side.

Alice retrieved the paper clip and tried again. Again it fell to the floor behind the table. She fished in her pocket, brought out a dime. The dime slid through and fell. So did a penny, and so did a ballpoint pen. Alice emptied her pockets into a pile on the other side of the table, and each item clattered to the lab floor, refused.

Alice went and gathered her belongings. One was missing. She searched the floor, frisked herself, reloaded her pockets, conducted an inventory. It was nowhere.

Lack had gobbled the key to our apartment.

12

In the weeks that followed it was as impossible to avoid updates on Lack's tastes as it was to catch a glimpse of Alice. Lack had swallowed an argyle sock, ignored a package of self-adhesive labels. He disliked potassium, sodium, and pyrite, but liked anthracite. He ate light bulbs, but disdained aluminum foil. Lack accepted a sheet of yellow construction paper, a photograph of the president, a pair of mirrored sunglasses. Lack went on a three-day hunger strike, refusing a batter's helmet, a bow tie, and an ice ax. He took a duck's egg, fertilized, refused a duck's egg, scrambled.

Some items were measured, weighed, evaluated, before going over Lack's table. Others were just giddily tossed across. Nobody understood Lack's system for choosing. He was consistent in never accepting something previously refused. Electric beater-blades tumbled off the table nine days in a row. He was inconsistent in sometimes growing bored with a previously favored item. The lists in the campus paper, under the heading *Lackwatch*, served as a daily dose of found poetry: hole punch, rosin bag, cue ball.

Everyone had a theory. We were all physicists now, thanks to Lack. Anyone could win the Prize—at least until the following morning, when some contradicting item was consumed. Lack seemed to have a fondness for disproving each new system of prediction at his first chance, as though theories themselves were to his taste.

Life went on. Pumpkins were purchased, mutilated, and left to rot on porches and windowsills. The team lost the Big Game. My hair grew out. Alice, living as she was "on the edge of the territory," was excused from teaching, and a graduate student took over her classes.

I missed her, terribly. I yearned, heart big and tender as a ripe eggplant. At the same time I played at indifference, my heart squeezed small and hard as an uncooked chestnut. The day she strolled into my office I felt my heart opt for chestnut size.

Her expression was gentle, her hair mussed into a halo. She took a seat across from me at my desk. I leaned back and compressed my lips, pretending she was a remiss student.

She looked past me to the bookshelves, the tattered notices and rusty thumbtacks that littered the walls. "I remember this office."

"You never came here," I said.

"I remember it. I sat here, you sat there."

"Maybe you picked me up here once. You never sat down."

50

"I sat while I waited. You had to finish something."

"I never work here. I can't imagine a time when I would have had something to finish in this office."

"I remember it."

"I hardly ever sit here, it's amazing you caught me here now. I was just coming in and sitting down for a minute. I certainly wouldn't just suddenly start finishing something here. It's a false memory."

"It doesn't matter, Philip. It still reminds me of you."

"Me sitting here now, you mean. Me sitting here now reminds you of me. I remind you of myself."

Alice sighed. I realized how angry I sounded.

"You threw away the food," Alice said.

"You were in the apartment?"

"I needed clothes. I was just looking around, and I saw the food was in the garbage."

"It went bad."

"Well, there's something about the apartment I wanted to talk to you about."

My heart twitched like a stone with a frog underneath. "Go ahead," I said.

"It's just sitting there. I can't use it right now, but I'm still paying rent."

"I'm still living there," I said bitterly.

"I know, Philip. But I keep wondering if you'd be better off with some company. So, when I suggest this you shouldn't just automatically say no. You should consider it. It would make me very happy."

"Who?"

"Evan and Garth. Just for a month."

"No."

51

"It's only a month. They're being kicked out and they didn't find another place."

Was she offering me a chance to even the score, to refuse her something? Or was it a test, to see if her charm could still sway me?

I felt my defenses leak away. It was a kind of masochistic thrill. Come back into my life, a part of me cried. Build an ant farm in the apartment, sprinkle German yeast. Anything. Just fill the lack there.

"I don't even know them," I said.

"They like you. They'll do the dishes, clean, cook. They go out during the day. You'll hardly see them."

"Go out where?"

"They wander around. Evan teaches braille three times a week. They go to the library. They go to their therapist."

"Together?"

"It's a special thing. They get paid for it. Some woman is studying them, the way they are, like those twins that make up private languages."

"Are they lovers?"

"I don't think so. They seem very interested in women."

"Women?"

"Not me, Philip. Just women, the idea of women."

I sighed.

"Say yes. It'll be good for all three of you."

"Bring them over and we'll talk about it." Come back to the apartment, I meant.

"We'll come by tonight."

"So you're still working with them, on seeing particles."

"Not exactly. I'm not really focused on that right now. But they got very excited, so I still give them things to do."

52

"You're more focused on Lack."

"Yes."

She got edgy. She didn't like the change of subject.

"How is Lack, then?" I asked.

"That's a silly question, Philip. Lack isn't *how.*"

"I thought your whole point was that he was. That he had a personality."

"Not a personality like 'how are you?' He doesn't have good days and bad days."

"You sound a little frustrated."

"I don't mean to lump you in with everyone else, but there's a degree of sensational interest—"

"He's a fad."

"Yes."

"It makes you feel protective. Possessive."

She recoiled at the last word. I suddenly saw how tired and frightened she was, her eyes rimmed with red, her cheeks sallow. I thought of her sleeping on a cot in the subterranean gloom, kept awake by the beeping detectors.

"Maybe I am," she said quietly.

13

Agreeing to think it over was the same as saying yes, of course. It brought Alice temporarily into the apartment, anyway. She ferried the blind men in and out with their belongings, cardboard boxes of utensils and condiments, heaps of braille magazines, black suits in dry-cleaner plastic.

Alice and I didn't talk, though. We listened to Evan and Garth. "Correction," Evan would say, "Tuesday, the appointment. The potluck dinner."

"There isn't any appointment Tuesday," Garth replied smugly. "It was moved to Wednesday. The application deadline was moved back a week. It has to be postmarked by midnight Thursday." Smiling mysteriously, his voice full of pride, he delivered the payoff. "The potluck dinner stands alone."

Alice and I were left alone just once, and then our talk was wound down, entropic.

"There are calls for you on the machine," I said.

"You mean the students with the tutorial thing?"

"Yes."

"I called them."

Silence. "So they have to be driven everywhere," I said. "The blind men."

"Only with their stuff. They take the bus."

"Or walk, I guess."

"Yes."

"The city is like a giant maze to them."

"Yes."

Silence. "You're listed in the winter catalog for a course called 'The Physics of Silence.' "

"Yes."

"Lack, I guess."

"Yes."

Her *yes* was a wall. I had lived inside the circle of Alice's silence, before. Now I stood utterly outside.

When Evan and Garth were installed she vanished again. The blind men took over, began redefining the apartment. Everything was knocked over, handled, repositioned. Dishes started piling up precariously, unrinsed, scabby with bits of egg, jam, and mustard. Briefcases full of braille were unpacked across the couch. Conversations rattled away over my head.

"What would you do if you found out I'd been lying to you?" said Garth suddenly.

Evan turned. "What do you mean?"

"What if I'd been lying about the precise location of certain objects?"

"Have you been?" Evan sounded a little panicky.

55

"What if I had? You'd be living in a world of my imagination. Huh. Think of that."

"We already discussed this. Ms. Jalter had a word for it. *Delusive conditioning.* It's not fair."

"I didn't say it was fair."

"Well, it's not."

Evenings Evan usually dug in with a braille physics textbook on the couch, while Garth sat on the guest-room bed and listened to his portable radio on headphones. I washed the dishes and paced onto the porch, to contemplate the night. I couldn't relax with them in the apartment. The blind men listened too hard. It made me too aware of my sounds, the scuffling of chair legs on hardwood, the flutter of turned pages. Each visit to the bathroom was a disaster, urine pounding into the bowl, ear-shattering flush.

If I'm lonely, I thought, I should at least be alone.

Lack, that week, refused a ski cap, a conical washer, and a pair of pinking shears. A curly lasagne, a twist of macaroni, a strand of nonskid spaghetti. A volume of Plutarch and a postcard of Copenhagen. A Robertson-tip screwdriver, a ball peen hammer, and a sundae spoon. Blueberries, oysters, calamine lotion. A photograph of the Rosetta stone, a gold-leaf cigarette case, and a concrete block. A lens cap, a hat tree, and a slice of chocolate cake.

He did, though, accept a slide rule, a bowling shoe, and an unglazed terra-cotta ashtray. A felt hat, a fountain pen, and a pomegranate. A Heritage Press reprint of *The Hunting of the Snark*, and an onyx replica of the Statue of Liberty. Pistachio ice cream in a porcelain dish. A bead of mercury.

Also a spayed female cat—a grizzled lab veteran, piebald from scratching at taped-on electrodes, named B-84.

14

B-84 had friends. They were massing angrily at the entrance of the physics complex, clogging the pathways, spilling out onto the lawn. The day was one of those California sports, summer in November, and I'd been strolling, avoiding my work. Then I met a student carrying a hand-lettered placard reading WHERE'S LACK'S HEART? I followed him to the rally.

The students who were only curious littered the fringes, exchanging disinformation. I pushed past them, to the front. The most defiant and outraged protesters were clustered under a bedsheet banner, unreadable except in fragments. UNIVERSITY, DOLLARS, RESPONSIBLE, DEATH. I threaded my way deeper into the crowd, to the base of the microphones. The grass under my feet was already torn.

The speaker was stringy and angular, his blond hair pulled

back in a ponytail, his plaid workman's shirtsleeves rolled up around his pale biceps. Journalism major, I guessed.

"We're obligated to demand an answer, to question this thing in our midst now. By all appearances it's a rampant scientific development, and we have to develop some consciousness, some overview, because it isn't being provided. We have the responsibility to ask some questions."

He stopped and peered out over his audience.

"The Lack is just a raping, uh, gaping rent in the fabric of the universe. It's been opened up right under our feet. The scientists can't even agree on it, there's disagreement in the scientific community, yet the experiments just go on. I for one think that maybe it's time we said wait a minute, let's have a serious look at this thing, decide what we have on our hands here, before we go throwing any more cats into it!"

Jeers of support from the crowd.

"The earth is just a small oasis in an endless desert of nothingness," he went on, encouraged. "We don't need more nothingness here on earth. There's plenty in outer space. If they want to study the Lack they don't have to bring it here to our campus."

"Send Lack back where he came from!" someone shouted from behind me.

"We want to send a message," said the student at the microphone. "We want to establish a forum where these issues can be properly debated. If the scientific community can't provide oversight in this case we'll be happy to provide it for them. We want to examine the Lack and any other development in the light of appropriate human values. That's all we ask."

Suddenly there was a bustling behind the banner. Some

kind of confrontation. The student at the microphone turned, and the public-address system issued a whine of feedback.

"What's going to happen, Professor Engstrand?" said a voice directly behind me.

I turned. The voice belonged to one of my students. I couldn't remember his name.

"It's the authorities, isn't it?" he said. "The science police."

"I don't know," I said.

Alice and her graduate student appeared at the microphone, looking small and out of place. Hardly the science police. Alice's student conferred with the protest leaders while Alice stood, gazing blankly over the crowd. She looked like a thing dragged unwillingly into the light. The brightness of the day was on the side of the protesters, and the cat.

Alice stepped up to the microphone, sweeping the hair back from her eyes. She didn't see me.

"I'd like to say a few things," she said. "This is a misunderstanding. You're creating a false dichotomy, something and nothing, life and entropy, the cat and Lack. We've been granted a chance to transcend those old distinctions. The void is making a gesture, trying to establish contact with life, trying to communicate with us. It would be tragic to turn down the offer. Lack is where life and entropy can reconcile their differences—"

The crowd began to boo.

You don't understand, I wanted to tell her. They're afraid. They're not like you, Alice. Not drawn to the void. They want insulation.

"Knowledge is very precious," she went on, quavering, defiant. She was playing the weakest card of a losing hand. "As precious as any living thing—"

She was drowned out in the booing, and though she went

on I couldn't make it out. The group behind her tried to retake the microphone. I shouldered my way to the front, got a footing on the nubby hillock where the microphone rested, and hoisted myself into the public eye.

I planted myself at the microphone and squinted out into the crowd, and past them, to the oblivious Frisbee throwers on the sun-drenched lawn. I was quiet for a long moment. I let authority gather on me like a crown.

"The universe is always swallowing cats," I said finally. "It's forever swallowing cats. There's nothing new here." I let a weariness creep into my voice, a tone I knew was infectious. "To protest it like this, in isolation . . . well, it's an act of enormous irrelevance. I'm touched, actually. There's a futile beauty to this gathering. Pick a death at random, come out in force."

Someone coughed.

"But it's a poor choice. There's a real confusion of symbolism here. Science, death, dollars. Lack isn't any of those things. Lack is a mistake, a backfire. He wasn't predicted, he's irksome. No military application. He's the human face poking back up out of the void, a pie in the face of physics. He's mixed up, he can't make up his mind. He likes pomegranates, except when he doesn't. My friends, Lack is here to help you take science less seriously."

The protest evaporated. The mob began to chatter, then wander away. Even as the students drifted off I felt their gratitude toward me. I'd relieved them of their unmanageable crusade. They could get back to skipping class.

I turned and saw Alice walking toward the entrance of the physics facility.

I chased her. She disappeared through the doors, but I caught her at the elevator, tapping impatiently at *down.*

60

"Alice." I was a little drunk with myself. "Alice, wait."

She stood facing the elevator.

I was panting. "Don't I deserve some thanks?" I said. "I did it. I broke up the lynch mob. Like Henry Fonda in *Young Mr. Lincoln.*"

She turned to me. Her expression was furious. "You want to make Lack yours," she said. "You think if you describe him he'll suddenly belong to you. Just like everything else."

The elevator doors opened and she stepped inside. I stared, struck dumb.

"But this time you're wrong," she said. "Lack is mine." The doors closed over her ravaged face.

15

I paced campus until dark, then stalked back to the apartment. When I saw the blind men were home I got into my car and drove off campus, found a bar, and deliberately had a drink with a woman.

An interesting woman, as it happened. She was dark-haired and tall, with a penetrating gaze and a smile that didn't show her teeth. She was sitting alone, sheltering a glass of red wine. I told her my name was Dale Overling, and asked if I could sit at her table. She said yes.

"You're not from the campus," I said.

"No."

"Not affiliated."

"No."

"Not a graduate of the school."

"No. No connection."

"You can't imagine how that turns me on."

"Buy me a drink."

The bar was tame and suburban, a fifties cocktail lounge not yet refurbished by student irony. It was nearly empty, a weekend place on a weeknight. I'd picked it for its distance from campus. But when I flagged the waitress it was a girl I recognized, a dizzy undergraduate, costumed in a yellow apron. Her eyes met mine and I froze her with a look of dread, willing her not to blow my cover.

"Take this wine away," I said. "Bring us drinks. Margaritas, salt on the glass. Bring us six of them. Line them up on the table."

"I can bring you a pitcher."

"I want a line of drinks. I want to see the glasses accumulate. Don't take away the empties, either."

She flickered away, pale and mothlike in the gloom.

"You're a very self-assured man, Mr. Overling," said my companion, her smile flickering.

"Dale, please. And you're a very perceptive woman, Ms. . . . ?"

"Jalter, Cynthia Jalter."

"May I call you Cynthia? You're a very perceptive woman."

"Thank you."

"I like to walk into a bar and find a perceptive woman sitting alone. It excites me. It doesn't happen that often."

"I'm flattered."

"And the fact that you're not from the campus, that takes it over the top. Because there's nothing that excites me quite like the idea of perceptive, intelligent women living in a university town *yet having no connection with the school.* Just living in the same town, right there, not needing to have anything to do with it. The idea of the intelligent woman in the university town. What is she? Why is she there? It's a stimulating idea.''

''You must be from the school.''

''Me? No, no. It's true, I'm visiting the campus, I'm a consultant. They fly me in. I spend a lot of time in towns like this, being flown in, flown out. I've got enough frequent-flyer points to send quintuplets around the world. But I hate these big university schools. They're big rotting carcasses. Rotten in the center. If I didn't just fly in, consult, fly out, I couldn't live with myself. As it is I take a hotel off campus, eat off campus, and go to bars and look for intelligent people who have nothing to do with the school. Those are the people to talk to in any situation. The ones on the edge, the outside.''

''Like me.''

''Exactly. They offer me a room on campus, you know. But I take a hotel. And I rent a big shiny car so I stand out. The American campus is crawling with these little brown and gray and buff-colored Peugeot cars and little Japanese cars. I get a big bright American car so they know I don't care. Bright red if I can.''

It didn't matter if Cynthia Jalter didn't believe me. At that moment Dale Overling was truer than I was. Heartier, more substantial.

''I sit in a bar in a different city three or four nights a week,'' I said. ''I always order the same things. I should write a guidebook. A browser's guide to tequila drinks in college towns.''

''Nonfiction bestseller list,'' said Cynthia Jalter. ''Position two, holding strong for months.'' Her smile was pursed.

''No. An underground guide, a photocopied thing. Little

tattered copies passed from hand to hand, with annotations, disagreements scrawled into the margins."

"Published under a pseudonym."

"Right. Professor X."

We drank. Mostly I drank. I needed to bolster the courage I'd already shown, as if it were borrowed in advance against future drinks. Cynthia Jalter sipped.

"Bigger gulps," I said. "There's a lot of drinks here."

She only smiled.

"Don't be smug. We're in this together. I can only run the show for so long, then I'm going to need your help. Drink up."

I finished one and put it aside, and took up the next. The sharp salt clung to my lip. I didn't bother wiping it away.

"You're probably wondering why I don't ask you what you do," I said. "The truth is I'd rather not know. It's probably something pretty dry, that's a safe guess. Despite your lack of connection to the school."

"It's a safe guess."

"And you'd rather not tell me, am I right? You like watching me do these verbal belly flops. And the more enigmatic you are, the farther out on a limb I have to go."

"You're right."

I raised my glass to her, then drank. The tequila was beginning to roil inside me.

"What's funny is I'm probably getting close. For example, I bet you're working with funding of some kind. A grant."

"Maybe."

"Yeah, you're definitely funded." I feigned disappointment. "It's all coming clear. Whatever you do wouldn't be possible without a major-league grant."

She laughed. The first time I saw her teeth, I think. "You're a very self-assured man, Dale."

"You said that already. You haven't said much, and you're already repeating yourself. I like the way you said my first name, though. Dale. I should say yours more. You're repeating yourself, *Cynthia.*"

"You're repeating yourself, Dale."

"Right. Very good. That's the kind of contribution I'll need from you from here on. Because I can't go on like this. It isn't possible. You're going to have to come down off your heavily funded pedestal and muck around in actual conversation with me here."

"I'll think about it."

"You're wondering how I sniffed you out about the grant. Well, I'm a consultant. I specialize in feasibility studies. Feasibility and viability, two very important words. To me they're like pronouns or conjunctions: he, she, it, and, or, feasibility, viability. So I just sensed the aura on you, the data accumulating."

I'd finished a margarita. I picked up another.

"This is actually very lucky for you, Cynthia. I could help you. I don't mean anything has to happen between us. I just mean because I feel like it, because I like the aura."

"Tell me more."

"I specialize in Nobel Prizes. Nobel consulting, I call it. Basically I come in, evaluate the work that's being done, and grade the Nobel potential. I help the client see what's holding it back, keeping it from breaking into Nobel-caliber work. No reason not to work with the Prize in mind. Anyway, that's my credo."

"It's fascinating," she said. Her smile was skeptical. But sweetly skeptical.

"For example, here in your town I'm involved in a real dilemma. What we have is a very viable experiment, something quite exciting Nobel-wise, and it's being headed up by a known quantity, a previous winner, in fact. But the project goes awry, turns up an unexpected result. It's still exciting work, but out of control. The Prize committee likes it clean and simple. They like you to come up with the result you predicted. So I've had to go in there and say, you're off the board, guys. You're no longer in Nobel territory. Good luck with the work, but I'm sorry. I don't feel it. I don't smell it. When I look at good work I can smell the Prize, I swear. And in this case, the aroma's evaporated."

At that moment my words went sour in my mouth. Invoking Lack, I'd brought Alice to mind.

I started measuring my distance from the exits.

"But enough about me," I said weakly.

Cynthia Jalter smiled, more sympathetically. She found my faltering charming. Dale was more likable tongue-tied. But in my drunken way I resented her now.

"Is something wrong?" she said.

"I'm fine. It's these damn flights. I'm all screwed up. It's four in the afternoon for me, or four in the morning. I should be running laps now, according to my schedule. Do you want to go outside and do some jumping jacks?"

"You don't look like you want to do jumping jacks."

"You'd be surprised." I opened the shirt button at my throat. Serious trouble was close.

"You look like something is worrying you."

"Actually, there's a woman, Cynthia. If you have to know. I'm a little torn up about it, I guess. That's why I wanted to meet someone intelligent and perceptive like yourself. I'm sorry it isn't working out. Maybe I need a glass of water."

67

"Stay there, Dale. I'll get you a glass of water."

"A glass water would be nice. Of."

I drank in a panic, both hands around the glass, hoping to dilute the contents of my stomach to digestibility. I felt heat and pressure building up in my rib cage. A fire or disaster inside. When I looked up from the glass I seemed to be peering through the eyeholes of a loosely fitted mask. I blinked, and the air was spangled with phosphenes.

"I'm in sort of a situation," I explained carefully. "My heart is being broken, very gradually, so I hardly notice it, even. I mean, it's difficult to pinpoint the exact moment it actually exactly happened. If it has yet."

"I'll drive you home," she said.

"Not home," I reminded her. "I wish I could remember the name of that damn hotel. All the same. Sunset . . . Mountainview? Bayview? Lodge? Inn? I thought I had a matchbook." I feigned a search, turned my pockets inside out, dropping change on the floor. "No such luck. Mountain Lion? Sea Lion? Are we near the mountains or the sea?"

Cynthia Jalter drove me home. She powered down my window from her place in the driver's seat, and the cool air whistled in my nostrils and blew tears out of my eyes horizontally, into my ears. I was silent, chagrined.

We pulled up outside my apartment. "Nice meeting you," she said. "Feel better. Don't forget your car."

"Rental job," I managed. "Let them find it. Fly out tomorrow." I tugged on the ashtray, the cushioned arm, the window handle, finally opened the car door and got out. "They put me up on campus here. Fly out tomorrow. Another day, another city."

"Give me a call sometime. I'm in the book. See you later."

"Never again, I'm sure. Thanks profusely for everything. Fly out tomorrow."

69

She drove away, leaving me there in the dark on my wobbly legs. I was surrounded by crickets. Lights burned in the apartment. The blind men were still awake. I tested myself, shook out my limbs, kneaded my numb jaw. I beat through the ferns to find the garden spigot, and splashed water on my face and down my collar. A toad groaned. I tiptoed back to the door.

When I went inside I found Garth, Evan, and Soft huddled around the couch. The lights in the room were dimmed. I focused, with difficulty, on the form across the couch.

Alice.

Her head was limp on the pillows, her hair splayed out, her forehead a pale beacon in the gloom. A blanket was tucked up to her chin. Were they admiring her, or mourning her? Or about to attack? I rushed over and saw her lips rippling gently with breath. Not dead.

I looked up at Soft. I must have looked a bit crazy, my eyes bugged and red, my collar wet.

"She's fine now, she's asleep," said Soft. "She needs rest. Where have you been?"

I thought for a minute. "I was involved in the demonstration," I said.

Soft frowned. I'm sure he thought I'd organized it. "I found her with Lack," he said. "After the riots this afternoon she locked herself in with him. They had to call me. I have the only other key."

"Why is she here, not the bed?"

"She's hard to carry," said Soft. "She passed out in the chamber. The recording devices were all shut off. So we have no way of reconstructing the events. I have some theories, though."

I leaned over, tucked her hair behind her ear, and put the

flat of my hand on her forehead. I felt a twist of shame. This was stolen intimacy, the first time I'd touched her in more than a month.

"I should go," said Soft.

He rolled his eyes to suggest that I should follow. We stepped out onto the porch together, leaving Garth and Evan, grim sentinels, to watch over Alice. Soft turned to me, his features drawn.

"She's no longer competent to manage the project," he said. "I'm looking at alternatives. But what's important is that she slow down. She needs to step back, get some perspective. I need your help. Don't let her spend any more nights in the lab. We've got students for that."

"I don't understand. What happened?"

"This business with the cat. Alice took it very personally. I don't know, I can only speculate, but I think she may have tried to enter Lack."

I stared at Soft. My face felt like Play-Doh receiving a footprint.

He nodded confirmation.

"Come see me in my office tomorrow," he said. "We'll talk more then."

He crossed the street to his car. I went inside. Alice was still asleep. Evan and Garth were pacing, busy doing nothing, like their first night in the apartment. Alice's return had unsettled them. Soft didn't know of my recent distance from her, but they certainly did. I imagine their alert noses had sniffed out the traces of my drinking, too.

"Professor Soft suggested that she stay here at night from now on," said Evan. "We certainly agree."

71

"We'd be happy to sleep in the guest room," said Garth. "Or out here if that's better."

"Take the guest room," I said.

"Good. And Philip?"

"Yes?"

Garth grew solemn, raised his chin, fixed his ungaze on some infinite distance. "Evan and I want you to know we'll do anything we can to help. You just have to ask."

"Thank you."

There was a pause, a leaden silence. "Huh," said Garth. "I suppose we'll go to bed now."

They scuttled into the guest room, and closed the door.

I knelt beside Alice, careful not to wake her. I could hear the blind men running water, brushing their teeth. Outside, crickets pulsed. I don't know how long it was that I sat there, silently contemplating her, tracking the flicker of dream state across her eyelids, the murmur of breath in her throat. Finally I spoke her name, and nudged her shoulder.

"Philip," she said.

"Yes."

"What happened?"

"Soft brought you here. Everything's okay. Come to bed."

She nodded, still asleep, really, and let me guide her to the bedroom. She stood wobbling and mole-eyed while I tugged the disarrayed blankets and sheets into shape, then she slid into the bed. When I switched off the overhead light she looked up at me meekly through the dark.

"Philip?"

"Yes?"

"Where are you going to sleep?"

"I'll sleep in the living room."

Reassured, she curled up and fell asleep.

I closed the door to the bedroom and patrolled the apartment on tiptoe. In the kitchen I scraped food off the blind men's plates and drank a glass of water. Then I remade the makeshift bed on the couch, stripped to my underwear, and put myself to bed.

But I didn't sleep.

The alcohol had leached out of my brain. But now I was drunk on Alice. She was back in the house. A miracle. I pictured her alone in the chamber, clambering onto the steel table to offer herself up to Lack's indifferent mouth. I shuddered. No wonder she couldn't love me anymore. She'd become estranged from humanness. She was on the brink of the void.

My heart pounded with fear. But she was safe for the moment. Safe in my bed. Under my care. I just had to make it last, keep her here. I'd draw her back to the human realm. I'd teach her human love again.

I couldn't afford any stupid mistakes. Any Cynthia Jalters. I had to walk the line. Be worthy.

Headlights from the road outside flared across the ceiling. In the kitchen the refrigerator hummed into midnight life. (I always imagine the light inside switching on, food cavorting.) My pulse slowed.

When I first heard the murmur I thought I was dreaming. But I opened my eyes, and it continued. Was it Alice, calling my name? I put aside the blankets, and crept out, cold and huddled, to the middle of the room, nearer the bedroom doors. The voices went on. I made myself still, to listen.

Evan and Garth arguing.

I went back to bed on the couch.

17

In the morning Evan and Garth vanished. I woke to see them breakfasting in decorous silence. I watched with half an eye as they tiptoed past me to the door. Then I went back to sleep, and a pleasantly forgettable dream.

An hour later I woke for real, to a hangover. I reconstituted myself in the bathroom with paste and swabs, drops and floss. I got a kettle boiling, its whistle-top propped open with a fork, shook coffee into a filter, and set out two cups. Evan and Garth had the cupboard stocked with a product called Weetabix. I opened a packet and poured milk over a desolate pod.

Alice padded in and sat at her place, not saying anything.

I gave her coffee, and we ate breakfast like mimes, yawning, stirring, and chewing in exaggerated silence. Alice hit the side of her cup with her spoon and spilled out a neat pylon of sugar. The room was washed with light. Alice's mussed hair was a backlit halo. We were a diorama labelled *Philip and Alice, Breakfast.* Circa two months ago. The past. Before.

"You slept about ten hours," I said. "From the time Soft brought you."

"It was Soft, then."

"Yes. He thinks you belong here. As far as he knows he was putting something back in its place."

She didn't say anything.

"He's worried about you," I said. "He says you're no longer competent to manage the project."

I decided not to make any *I* statements. We would talk about Soft's perceptions, Soft's concerns. Or Alice's. But not mine.

"There isn't any project," she said. "Just Lack. Lack and approaches to Lack. Soft's holding on to the idea of a project. That's his big blind spot."

"Soft's concerned about your approach to Lack," I said coolly. "He feels your approach is too, um, direct."

She looked down into her coffee. The sun sculpted hollows of light in her tired features. Tender feelings rustled in me like bat wings unfolding.

"He thinks you're identifying too much," I said. "Losing that essential detachment."

She looked up sharply. "Lack doesn't require detachment. That's Soft's error. Lack requires engagement, a relationship. It's something I was able to rise to. Soft is out of his depth."

"You're saying that what Lack wants is a relationship." I said, still calm.

"Right."

"And you're saying you can provide that."

"Right."

75

"A human relationship."

"Right."

I lost my cool a little. "He isn't getting one in you, Alice. You're moving away from the human. Lack is too powerful an influence, can't you see? He's changing you. You're becoming a void to match. You're not human if you're no longer able to *love.*"

I caught myself before I added the word *me.*

"Love isn't the problem," she said weakly. "I'm not having a problem loving."

"What are you saying?"

"You still don't understand, do you? Why I can't be with you anymore."

Don't address me, I wanted to say. Philip isn't here. This is Omnipotent Voice you're speaking with.

"You're in love with someone else," I heard myself say.

"Yes."

A change came over me, a phase transition. A flush rose through my chest and neck.

"You're in love with Lack," I said.

"Yes."

Should I have known sooner?

Love is self-deception, remember. And my competition was so improbable.

But now that it was named, Alice's Lack-love seemed obvious, a foregone conclusion. Probably the whole campus buzzed with it, and I was the last to know.

"The way you loved me?" I squeaked.

"No. Yes."

I studied her. She sat with a leg up on the chair, her hair wild, her eyes glowing from tired sockets. Her mouth was drawn defiantly tight. Her Lack-love was real, I saw. She looked crushed under the weight of her impossible love. I felt an admiration, despite myself.

"Does anyone else know?"

"I hadn't even admitted it to myself until just now." A tear painted a reflective stripe down her cheek.

"Does Soft?"

"You would know better than I would."

Yes, Alice had been living on the brink of the void, but it wasn't some singular, icy, inhuman place. In fact, the same void yawned out underneath me, too. Unrequited love.

It seemed reasonable to call hers unrequited. If Alice had really climbed up on Lack's table, then he'd turned her down, hadn't he? Making things disappear was the only *I love you* in his binary vocabulary.

Had she, though? I was afraid to ask. Instead I got up and cleared the dishes into the sink. I wanted to buy a plane ticket, fly away, make my claims to Cynthia Jalter true. Leave my colleagues with a mystery. Professor X.

In the sink the coffee grounds rose up, swirling out of the bottoms of our cups, and were washed down the drain.

"All this time down there," I said, not facing her. "You were slipping away from me. Feeling communion with this thing, unable to talk about it."

"Yes."

I realized, too late, that I'd used a forbidden pronoun. *Me.* Distracted, I'd pled guilty to possession of a self.

"So it's simple, then," I said. "No mystery. You don't love me because you love Lack."

"Yes."

"But he doesn't love you back."

"Yes."

"You tried, then. You offered yourself."

No answer. But when I turned from the sink she stared at me hollowly, and nodded.

18

"We've drifted a long way past physics here, Philip. I'd like to try to get us back on course."

Soft's office was surprisingly intimate. It was easy to imagine it as a blown-up model of the interior of his skull. The walls were lined with texts, a decade's issues of *Physics Letters* and *Physical Review*. The desks were heaped. On the wall was a water-stained certificate, subtly crooked inside its frame. Yellowing fireproof ceiling, ancient fluorescent desk lamp. Soft always seemed reptilian inside the physics lab, and out of place everywhere else, but this office was an intermediate, a human space he could credibly inhabit.

Soft sat behind his desk. In the rotting chair to his right sat an Italian physicist, just off the plane. He was tall and ruddy, and wore a wrinkled, lemon yellow suit. His collar was open and his tie was bundled into his jacket pocket, where it stuck out like a tongue. Soft introduced him with a name that began morphing so crazily the moment I heard it—Crubbio Raxia? Carbino Toxia? Arbino Cruxia?—that I didn't dare try to say it aloud.

He sat watching me intently while Soft spoke.

"We're dividing up the Lack hours," Soft said. "I'm reclaiming a portion of the schedule myself. A team of our graduate students has submitted an impressive proposal, and they'll be awarded a shift. Most exciting to me personally is the exchange we've negotiated with the Italian team. Carmo and his staff will be given access to Lack, in return for a share of hours at their supercollider in Pisa, something we've craved for years. Lack is a considerable bargaining chip."

The Italian pursed his lips. "We have been following your results very closely. It is important work. Cannot be monopolized, you see? The international community has claims."

"Carmo's team has some very interesting theories, and they're eager to put them to the test."

"Hah! Yes. It's a very narrow interpretation, so far."

Soft winced. The Italian's enthusiasm obviously irritated him. Maybe there was a political side to this exchange, some debt being paid.

"The reason I called you here," continued Soft, "is that I'd like to ask you to administer Professor Coombs' hours. Be her, ah, chaperone. I wouldn't dream of disrupting her work, but I am looking to tighten up our sense of procedure here. I want to develop a variety of approaches, foster a little give-and-take among the various teams. And naturally there's going to be some downtime, when one team is breaking down equipment or cleaning up the observation area. There's only one Lack. So we're all going to have to move forward in a spirit of cooperation. I'm looking to you, Philip, as someone who's really an expert on how we do things around here, to help apply the subtle brakes and levers that can make this thing go. Especially with Professor Coombs. Because it's not an easy thing, but in effect we're downgrading her status in this situation, cutting into her time. Not that there aren't compensations, of course, but still. I'm sure you're cognizant of my drift."

Soft smiled at Carmo—Texaco? Relaxo? Ataxia?—and folded his hands across his desk.

"But Alice—" I began.

"I don't think this is really the time and place and time to talk about Professor Coombs' recent difficulties, Philip. Professor Braxia isn't interested in our petty little disputes or eccentricities. There's a difference of opinion between myself and Professor Coombs. That's no secret, I'm not hiding that from the Italian team. The point is to open this thing up to a variety of approaches."

"We are not coming in here blind," said Braxia smoothly. "We know your Professor Coombs' work. She is passionate, stubborn. We like that, we understand that."

"I think it goes somewhat beyond that," I said. "Alice's feeling is that we're past traditional approaches here. That this is more along the lines of, say, alien contact, first contact, and that we ought to have a heightened sensitivity to, uh, anthropological or exobiological concerns. I think she's likely to object to a strenuously hard-physics approach at this point. Speaking as her representative here."

I was winging it. Stalling. But if Soft wanted to come between Alice and Lack, did I really want to stand in the way? My wishes and hers weren't necessarily one and the same.

Carmo Braxia stretched back in his seat, and crossed his leg over his knee. "My dear fellow. It's extraordinary to me that you would oppose an exercise of the basic scientific rigorousness that the situation is demanding. Just, for example, setting up a sonar or light beam to try and bounce a signal off the interior surface of this Lack. No damage is risked. Why has this not been attempted?"

"I'm afraid he's right, Philip. There's a basic threshold of responsibility here. We're currently below it."

"Perhaps there is a corresponding Lack, an out-hole," suggested Braxia excitedly. "Undiscovered somewhere. Spewing out the junk you push into your end here. In some third-world nation perhaps. Hah! Very American."

"Professor Coombs will have her time," said Soft. "She'll have plenty of chances to vindicate her theories. We're all going to stay open and receptive. We'll all pursue our own conclusions. At some point the teams will converge on the actual truth. We'll know what we're looking at here."

"Results," said Braxia gravely.

"And so you need my help with Alice," I said.

Soft winced again. He wanted me to call her *Professor Coombs*. "More than that," he said. "We're inviting your presence. Work closely with Professor Coombs, with Carmo and the Italians, with myself, and look for correspondences we're missing. Things we're too close to see. Your kind of thing. And use your influence to keep Professor Coombs on an even keel. Focused, but not . . . obsessive."

Braxia had pulled a tuft of stuffing out of the torn arm of his chair and was holding it up quizzically to the light.

"What if I were to submit a competing claim for time," I said, improvising. "Representing, say, the concerns of the interdisciplinary faction. Sociological, psychological, even literary concerns. I'd represent the community of the bewildered, the excluded. I think yesterday's demonstration proves the existence of my constituency. Would that be compatible with your time-share format?"

Soft looked like he was trying to swallow his Adam's apple. "I see no problem there," he managed to say. "Put in your claim. We'll run it through the usual review process."

"What's important, my dear fellow, is that we get some physics done. We understand your Professor Coombs is feeling unwell. We extend our best wishes. Until she is ready to utilize her time we propose to offer a further exchange." Braxia rustled in his pockets, pulled out a single folded sheet, and opened it. "For every additional weekly hour past the initial allotment," he read, "one additional square foot of observation space in the Pisa facility. After an additional ten hours weekly, the rate changes to six additional inches per additional square hour."

"I don't think Alice will consider any concessions."

"Here." Braxia handed me the paper. "You will have our offer at hand. That is all I ask. The exchange is no concession. We have a very desirable facility—ask Soft. Four thousand events per run. A very nice machine. Explain it to him, Soft."

"They have a very nice machine," said Soft. "The envy of the international community."

"Not anymore," I said.

19

Soft had Lack's chamber sealed off during the reorganization, leaving Alice to founder in the apartment. She never went out. I would come home to find her dazedly channel-surfing, or stirring a can of condensed chowder to life on the stove, or fallen asleep on the couch, a notepad clutched to her chest, pages blank. We didn't talk. We avoided each other. I slept on the couch and was awake and out of the house before she even stirred. She and the blind men dined together, I ate separately. The apartment was a museum of unspoken words.

Finals were faintly visible on the event horizon, and students began making pilgrimages to my office to ask about their status, negotiate extra-credit assignments, beg extensions on work already due, or plead for outright mercy. I started pinning notes to my door. I employed the uncertainty principle, offered only fleeting glimpses of my trajectory. The coffee machine, second floor, between three-fifteen and three-twenty, Wednesday. Walking across the east lawn toward the parking lot, eleven-forty-five, Monday. With correction fluid I shortened my phone number in the posted directories to six digits.

The Italian team appeared, led by Braxia. They took over a table in the far corner of the faculty cafeteria, chattering in the incomprehensible double language of Italian and Physics. Lack-watch vanished, or was suppressed. Soft's stature was restored. He could again be seen striding through hallways like a comet with a tail of students, his brow knit, his finger cutting a swath through the air.

That morning forest fires to the north produced a carpet of ash that reddened the skies. The sun glowed orange in the east, an eerie morning sunset. The gray flecks settled in a fine coat over windshields, automatic teller machines, and public art. The entire day was dusk. When night finally came it was like a benediction.

In the parking lot after the day's class, the flakes still falling like snow, I felt oddly peaceful. I thought of Alice and the blind men affectionately. Forgivingly. I decided to drive home and share a meal with them, instead of going to a restaurant. So I drove to a liquor store, the flakes lit like movie-theater smoke in the beam of my headlights, and bought a bottle of red wine as evidence of my good intentions.

But when I jogged up the porch steps and went inside I found the blind men in a tizzy. Alice had left the apartment, for the first time since Soft's rescue.

"She was supposed to be here," Evan said. They were both dressed up in their jackets and hats. Their canes were ready. They wore expressions of exaggerated dismay, jaws clenched, noses wrinkled. "She said she'd drive us. And now she isn't even here."

"Where'd she go?" I said, confused. "Drive you where?"

"Therapy," said Evan.

"Huh," said Garth. "If we knew where she was she'd be *here*, and we'd be gone already. You wouldn't be talking to us."

"She said, 'I'll see you back here at five-thirty.' " said Evan. " 'I'll give you a lift.' Her exact words. It is five-thirty, isn't it?"

Garth smacked at his watch. "Five-forty-seven."

"That's seventeen minutes late," Evan pointed out, his voice rising. "It is Thursday, isn't it?"

I stood holding my bottle of wine.

"My watch could be wrong," Garth mused. "But it's certainly Thursday. That much I know."

Evan felt at his watch. They were going to conduct a survey of all tangible objects and irrefutable facts at hand. I stepped in.

"Oh, look," I lied. "Note on the refrigerator." I craned my neck and squinted, pretending to read from a distance, fooling some invisible spectator. " 'Philip,' " I pretended to quote, " 'will you give E. and G. lift? Emergency meeting. Don't worry. Alice.' So there's your answer. Don't worry. I'll drive you."

Why the ruse, when I could have suggested the ride as my own idea? Easy. I yearned for something as normal and domestic as a note on the refrigerator. Alice had never left me a note on the refrigerator.

Also, I was staking my claim as sole worrier, shutting the blind men out of this current crisis. Alice's new disappearance would be all mine. Not Evan and Garth's, not Soft's.

I helped them into my car, digging seat belts out from between seats. Evan gave me directions. It wasn't far. My wipers cleaned a window out of the newly fallen ash, and we took off, in silence.

My thoughts were with Alice. I was pretty sure I knew where she was.

But she couldn't get into the chamber. I had the key. Soft had given it to me.

"Is time subjective or objective?" said Garth from the backseat, his voice droning in the darkness.

Evan and I were silent.

"I mean, if my watch says five-thirty, and I go around all day believing in that, and then I run into you and your watch says five o'clock, half an hour difference, and we've both gone around all day half an hour different—your two, my two-thirty, your four-fifteen, my four-forty-five, half an hour in the past relative to me, and certain of it, just as certain as I am, and we begin arguing, and then, at that moment, the rest of the world blows up, huh, just completely disappears, and we're all that's left, there's no other reference point, no other *observer*, and for me it's five-thirty and for you it's five, isn't that a form of time travel?"

"Time travel?" said Evan.

"Five o'clock is successfully communicating with five-thirty," said Garth.

We pulled up in front of the address Evan had given me. It was an ivy-covered brick house, lacking a shingle or plaque to identify it as a proper site of therapy. The blind men clambered out. I followed, feeling protective. What sort of therapy was this, anyway? Evan and Garth could be duped into all kinds of abuses. Having fooled them five minutes before with the refrigerator-note gag, I knew how vulnerable they were. I'd go and meet this therapist. Then back to rescue Alice.

87

Garth rang the bell. A buzzer sounded and we stepped into a carpeted, high-ceilinged foyer. It smelled faintly musty. Garth turned a doorknob at the right, and he and Evan went in to a consulting room that was reassuringly bland and clean, free of instruments of torture.

As I peered in after them a voice behind me spoke my name. I wheeled to find Cynthia Jalter, holding a jet-black clipboard, still tall, still darkly attractive, still smiling knowingly.

She looked in at the blind men, who nodded together at the sound of her step, then shut the door, isolating us two in the foyer.

"I didn't mean—," I said.

"I understand," she said. "You didn't know. You were just dropping them off."

"Yes," I said, slowly grasping that this wasn't the wrong house, wasn't some dream or practical joke. Cynthia Jalter was their therapist.

"You pay them to come here," I recalled, inserting it in the place of a thousand apologies.

"They couldn't possibly afford it themselves," she said. She stood, her back to the consultation room, her clipboard hugged to her chest, eyeing me curiously. "I'm well funded, as you guessed the other night, Philip."

"Your research is into blindness, then."

"Coupling," she said. "Obsessive coupling."

"Ah. The way they are together, you mean. The private world. Twins, invented languages, that sort of thing."

"Yes."

"You help them separate, I guess. A Siamese-twin surgeon of the soul."

"I help them understand it," she said. "They can make

their own choices. The goal is to develop an awareness, from inside, of how dual cognitive systems form, how they function, how they respond to hostile or contradictory data. Threats to stability, inequal growth by one member. Cognitive dissonance. I'm sure these concepts are familiar."

"Oh, yes."

"In the larger sense my research is into the delusory or subjective worlds that exist in the space between the two halves of any dual cognitive system. It applies to any coupling, from obsessive twins all the way down to a chance momentary encounter in public, between two strangers."

"Ah."

"The therapy can serve as a catalyst for change, sure. As the inherent limitations of two-point perspective are exposed. It's inevitable. But the research is pure. Perhaps sometime we'll have a chance to talk at length."

"Oh, yes." I said this stupidly, too fast.

"Good." Her smile was wry.

"You knew my name, just now," I said. "Not the fake name from the bar. Dale Overling."

"Evan and Garth—we talk about their situation, too. Daily life stuff."

"So you knew it was me, the other night."

"Not right away," she said. "But it dawned on me. And I drive them home sometimes. So when I dropped you off, I knew for sure."

I wanted to flee. I felt like an idiot. Anyway, I had to go search for Alice, rescue her.

"We're keeping Evan and Garth waiting," I said.

Her smile was knowing. "You have somewhere to go."

"Actually, yes."

She straightened, and lifted her clipboard as if to weigh it. She looked at me and I saw that she had science gaze. The look that seemed to encompass my whole life inside theoretical brackets. Paradigm Eyes.

Alice used to freeze me with that look. Before she lost it, surrendered it along with everything else, to Lack.

"Well, I hope we get that chance to talk," she said, still smiling.

"Right." I was panicked. I thought of last time, my jaunt from the apartment while Soft dragged Alice home. Why was I always with Cynthia Jalter at these moments? Alice's vanishing belonged to me this time, if I hurried. I had to go claim it.

"And Philip?"

"Yes?"

"I know about Alice. They talk about her."

"And Lack?"

"And Lack."

I winced. I didn't want Cynthia Jalter to take a professional interest. The possibility that she might view Alice and me, or worse, Alice and Lack, as a fascinating and absurd example of obsessive coupling was horrifying.

And yet here I was, rushing away to attend a new phase of the crisis. I felt exposed.

"Well," I said. "I hope you take all they say with a grain of, as the saying goes, salt."

"Yes."

"I have to go. You'll drive them home, I guess."

"Yes."

"Oh, good." I slipped back through the front door, then

ran stumbling down the porch steps and back to my car. I was panting, as if after some vast exertion. I seat-belted myself into place with difficulty, my fingers numb.

Dual cognitive system?

Two-point perspective?

New data, threats, unequal growth?

I drove back to campus, to the parking lot of the physics facility.

20

Alice sat, slumped, elbows on knees, against the padlocked doors of Lack's chamber. She was a human mite in the machine, an insect sucked up in a vacuum cleaner. Her head was ducked between her shoulders, blond hair shining in the dim, steely light of the corridor. She looked up forlornly when she heard me coming.

"Alice." I panted. "I'm here."

"I see."

"You're okay."

She smiled. "Yes."

"So." I peered around the curve of the hallway. We were alone. The doors to the lab were still locked, and I had Alice's copy of the key. "So, I guess you're just waiting here, huh?"

"I guess."

"Sort of staking out a position, is that it? An encampment?"

"I don't know, Philip."

"Resting. A siesta."

"If you like."

I sagged. The air had gone out of my rescue already. Alice stared at me, plainly resenting the intrusion.

"Well, I think we need to talk."

"We could talk in the apartment."

"But that's just it," I said, trying to get some momemtum. "We never do."

"You came here to talk?"

I concealed my panting. "Yes." I slumped down across from her, against the opposite wall, one knee up, the other leg stretched out. If she'd taken the same position our feet could have touched across the width of the corridor. The fluorescent light above us flickered and blinked. "I want to pin some things down."

"What things?"

"You love Lack. The way you used to love me, but don't anymore."

She sighed. "You keep repeating it, Philip."

"Then it's true."

"Yes. I love Lack." She didn't flinch or falter. She was comfortable saying it now.

"I was too real for you. You wanted to meet someone imaginary."

"Lack is real, Philip. He's a visitor. An alien."

"Lack's an idea, Alice. He's your projection."

She stared at me defiantly. "Well, he's a much better idea

than a lot of others I can think of. He's the idea of perfection, the idea of love, of perfect love."

"Love of pomegranates, you mean. Love of slide rules."

"Love of what Lack loves, yes. Pure love."

"He's gobbling things, Alice. That's all. Even if you're guessing right, even if he's loving them, what does that have to do with you? Why is that something to fall in love with?"

"It's a basic response to something alien," she said. "Lack comes here, seeking contact, one hundred percent receptivity, and I have the same impulse in return. To embrace the alien. Why can't you understand? It's a very high-minded thing. I'm an evolutionary paragon, Philip. And you would be too. I know you well enough. If it had been you in my place you'd be in love."

"I am in love," I said, with a defiance of my own.

I thought about the key in my pocket, unknown to Alice. For all her talk she was stuck out here in the chilly corridor, locked out of the room where the object of her desire rested in darkness, silence, indifference.

"So you're sitting here in the cold, an evolutionary paragon," I said.

"The first shift is at midnight," she said quietly. "The Italian team. That's when Soft opens it up. I wanted to be here."

"Like a teenager on line for front-row seats."

She didn't speak. Maybe she flushed—it was hard to tell in this light.

"You know I've been asked to administer your lab time," I said. "Soft's worried about what you'll do with Lack."

"What are you trying to say?"

"I don't know. I mean, I couldn't care less about Soft. Under normal circumstances I'd prefer your approach. If it didn't involve the love thing."

"And under these circumstances?" she said, harsh, unrelenting.

Our eyes locked. Hers fierce, mine searching.

"I want to be your friend," I said.

No reply.

"Forget what went before," I said. "It doesn't matter. You need support. That's obvious."

Her eyes were still hard. "I can't believe you all of a sudden understand about Lack."

"Well, I'm not sure I'm going to help you climb up onto the table and disappear. But understand the feelings, generally, yes."

She looked at me warily. She brushed her hair back, and I saw her chin was trembling. "I'm under a lot of pressure right now, Philip."

"I understand."

"The kind of friend I need now is one who doesn't put a lot of demands on me. Someone I wouldn't have to answer to or make justifications to, or even necessarily see or talk to when I didn't want to."

"Right," I said.

"I don't have room for anything else in my life right now."

"Right."

I couldn't keep from thinking, she wants me to be as invisible as Lack. If I left her completely alone she would do me the favor of *envisioning* me as her friend. Another one of her theoretical cohorts.

As I sat there, smiling weakly at Alice, the two of us bracketing the empty space of the hallway, I hallucinated vividly that we were in the bowels of some vast interstellar vehicle, a futuristic ark that had fallen into disuse yet still drifted through the gulf of stars, and that we had lost our way, Alice and I, in our search for the control room. Or found it securely locked, like Lack's chamber. That this vast drifting thing we were so helpless to command had, somewhere, an ignition key, a steering wheel. But we couldn't find them.

The vision faded. Once upon a time I would have described it to Alice.

"You want me to go, don't you," I said. "I'm not helping, I'm not even entertaining you. You want me to leave."

She nodded in a helpless way.

"I can't possibly compete. I could never offer you as little as Lack does. He's playing hard to perceive."

Alice stared at me through red-rimmed eyes.

"I'll just leave you down here," I said. "Crying alone in this place. I'll go back to the apartment and be alone there, in the same state. Alike, but exiled from each other, islands of misery. You down here and me up there."

"Evan and Garth are there," she said.

It wasn't cruel humor. She honestly thought they were a consolation.

"They're—," I almost said Cynthia Jalter's name. "They're at their therapist's."

We were both crying. Invoking the blind men, and the apartment, had drawn us back to earth somehow, out of the searing, empty sky of our pain. That plain configuration of rooms and beds. Finally there were always objects—the car and the apartment, Lack's tuning forks and terra-cotta ashtrays, the blind men's clattering canes—ballast to drag us away from the void.

"Philip, hold me."

I crawled across the margin of floor and held her. I put my arms around her shoulders, my face in her hair. We cried together. Our bodies made one perfect thing, a topological whole, immutable, complete, hollows turned to each other, hollows in alliance. We made a system, a universe. For a moment.

Then I left her to her vigil. I went to pace the campus, to be under the stars, fog, and pollution with my thoughts, circling only gradually on the apartment. By the time I got back to my couch Evan and Garth were returned from their therapy, and peacefully asleep.

"Well, you've got a case," said the radio talk-show host. "No problem there. But if you sue her you lose the relationship. I haven't seen the marriage that could survive litigation."

"I was afraid you'd say that," said the caller.

I was on the couch, still in yesterday's clothes. I'd kicked my blanket onto the floor in the night, and tugged the sheet up in a bunch around my neck. The radio was playing in the guest bedroom.

The blind men were in the kitchen running water, clanking silverware, cooking what smelled like glue. I crept to the door and slipped out, not wanting to explain Alice's absence to them. I couldn't face them in the dead, used-up space of the apartment. From outside I peered in and saw Evan poking questioningly at the bedclothes on the couch. I ran.

The day was cold and bright. I crossed the lawns, retracing

my steps. I'd slept badly. I was sealed in a pocket of leftover night, mouth dry, eyelids swollen.

I went back to the physics facility. Now the hallways bustled with students, their hair wet from the shower, mauling bagels or croissants as they hurried to check the outcomes of overnight experiments. Instruments that had been quiet the night before beeped and blinked at me, as though they'd detected an inauthentic presence. I was a bit of the night myself, haunting the new day. Garth would have called me a time traveler.

Lack's outer doors were open. Phase two had started. I went inside. I was alone in the observation room. The overhead screen was dead. The blinds were down over the window to the Cauchy-space lab. I levered them open, and there was Alice in the intermediate zone, the clean room. She had her back to me. Her face was pressed against the glass of the window to Lack's chamber.

Inside, Braxia and the Italian team frenziedly set up their equipment, a galaxy of cameras, detectors, shields, counters, and meters, a forest that overwhelmed Lack's little table. I raised my hand to tap at the glass, to draw Alice's attention, then stopped.

What would I say to her?

So I watched. Watched Braxia command his efficient team, and watched Alice watching, leaning on her elbows, her devotion to Lack absolute. She must have hated to see him swarmed over by the Italians. We made a pyramid, Braxia observing Lack, Alice observing Braxia and Lack, myself observing all three. I thought: If Alice still feels my eye tracks, she'll turn. She didn't. I shut the blinds and went out of the facility.

My first class was at three. I needed a shower and a shave before then. Maybe a nap. But if I killed some time the blind men would go out. I could have the apartment to myself. I raised my collar against the morning wind and hiked up the sunny path to the soccer fields. Practice was underway.

My graduate student had applied for funding to study the geographic spray of athletes on a playing field following an injury. He wanted to understand the disbursement of bodies around the epicenter of the wounded player, the position of the medics and coaches, and the sympathy or skepticism implicit in the stances chosen. All taking into account the seriousness of the injury, the score in the match when it occurred, the value of the player injured. Et cetera. I'd written an effusive letter in support of the application. The work had been funded generously. My student was here now on the sidelines, jotting notes on a clipboard as he watched the players sprint. I moved up beside him.

The players on the sidelines jogged in place, cold in their shorts, skin red and goose-pimpled, tousled hair glinting in the late-November sun. They were used to seeing my student by now, but they seemed wary of me. The coach straddled the line, barking orders, slapping at the men as they joined the drills.

"Subjects who express sympathy at a teammate's fall are sixty-eight percent likelier to sustain a treatable gravity-related injury in the same game," my student said, not looking at me, his eyes trained on the field.

"That's good work," I said.

"Subjects who assume a sympathetic posture at an opponent's fall are another sixteen percent likelier."

"Very good."

We were like athletes ourselves, perfecting a purely meaningless activity, ears growing numb in the wind. I felt a solidarity with the players. I wanted to sustain a treatable gravity-related injury myself. I tested my weight surreptitiously, faked a limp.

100

It was good to see my student so busy doing what I'd taught him to do. Looking for the hidden data, the facts that hide inside obvious things. The interdisciplinary dark matter. And a protégé confirmed my existence in the world. I felt grateful. I wanted to share some kernel of advice with him, some warning about women, but nothing came to mind. It was okay. We were safe here, on the sidelines, far from danger.

So we watched the players drill. Passing the ball, rolling it backward with their toes, popping it up with their knees and foreheads. Running patterns, in bursts of speed, then falling away. The goalies lunged from side to side, protecting the sanctity of the delineated space. And when a defenseman shot suddenly upward, then fell groaning to the ground, players around him freezing, assuming revealing postures, the ball rolling to a stop unmanned, my student and I rushed together onto the field, huffing, experts who'd been waiting in abeyance for the right time to assume their roles, and had a closer look.

22

Alice's first shift began at noon, three days later. Soft had reassigned her the key, after extracting solemn promises. Still, I meant to be there. I spent the morning in my office attempting to make good on my threats to Soft, drawing up and discarding a series of mediocre proposals for use of Lack-time, getting nowhere. Faced with Lack I became Lack-like myself. I had nothing to say, no experiment to conduct. I wanted to represent the needs of those baffled and helpless before Lack, but I resembled my own constituency too closely.

So I sat crumpling sheets of paper. The problem was that my usual approach—anthropology—would give blessing to Alice's anthropomorphization of Lack. I wanted to prove Alice wrong, to show Lack to be a dead thing, a mistake, a cosmic pothole. But the physicists were in charge of that. So I ground to a halt, let my pen hand fall to the desk. And looked up at the clock.

Late.

I was late for Alice's first shift. Potential disaster. Did I want her to throw herself in? I ran from my office, and across campus, to the physics facility. Eyes bulging with terror, I made my way down in the elevator, to Lack's suite. The doors were locked. I pounded on them.

This would be a magnificent rescue. Or a tragic near miss.

Nothing. I pounded again.

The handle turned, with a calmness that was an admonishment. Braxia's florid face appeared.

"Hello," he said. "You would like to come in."

"Yes."

"By all means, dear fellow. Come in."

The lights were off in the observation room. The equipment was quiet. Braxia led me through to Lack's chamber, which was lit. Most of the Italian team's various monitors were folded away into the corners of the room. Lack's table was spotlit in the center of the floor, alone. Laid out on wax paper on the near side of it was a sandwich and a green plastic supermarket basket of strawberries.

Braxia turned to me, looking vaguely menacing in the shadows. "It's nice in here now, no?" he asked.

"Yes," I said, panting, surely bright red.

"Well. So. An unexpected visit, eh?"

"It's Professor Coombs' first shift," I said. "Where is she?"

He folded his arms and looked at me appraisingly. The corners of his mouth twitched into a smile.

"Where is she?" I said again.

"She came already and went already," said Braxia. "You missed her."

For one deranged moment I imagined that Braxia had committed some act of violence. Lack, the perfect murder weapon. I took an involuntary step backward before I regained my poise.

Braxia turned to the table, and picked up a neat triangle of sandwich. Mayonnaise glistened in the spotlight. "You're very worried about her, I gather," he said.

"I'm supposed to administer her shift."

"Watch over her, you mean. Because of Soft's concern."

"Yes."

"Well, Soft asked me to do the same. So here I was. No problem."

"Soft asked you to watch Alice?"

Braxia smiled disingenuously. "Yes, my dear fellow, he did." He bit off the corner of the half-sandwich, then fit the rest of it back into place on the wax paper.

"Well," I said, feeling a bit testy, "he asked me to watch over you *and* Alice. To keep an eye on you both."

Braxia bowed slightly, a subtle folding at the waist. "Very good," he said. "That's better, I admit. I will now have to petition to Soft to be permitted to watch over you as well."

He smiled again. I was unnerved by his breezy amiability. The blithe way he stood chewing his sandwich while I panted.

"Well, what happened?" I said finally.

"Oh. What happened. She came in here, asked to be alone, so I went outside. It was about five minutes, and she came out. Crying. And she went away. That's all." He picked up his sandwich, took another bite.

"You didn't go in with her?"

"No. I respect her privacy."

"So you don't know what happened."

He shrugged. "I have a guess. But no."

I was envious. Another man had acted as Alice's protector in this chilly subterranean theater.

Braxia stared at me, plainly amused. "What's the matter?" he said.

"Nothing."

"Nothing? My dear fellow, you look like shit. I'll tell you what is the matter with you. You are worried that Professor Coombs, Alice, is going to put herself up here"—he slapped at the table—"and that's it, no more Professor Coombs."

"Yes," I admitted.

He smiled again. "Come here," he said.

I stepped up, unexpectedly fearful, to the table. It was the nearest I'd been to Lack, though I'd certainly been nearer in nightmares.

Braxia put his hand on my shoulder, coaxed me up even closer. I moved forward and put my hand on the smooth, cool surface of the table. Braxia slid his sandwich to one side, leaving the strawberries where they sat.

"Look," he said. He took a ring off his left hand and hid it in his fist, then slowly moved the hand with the ring forward, across the space of the table, past the point where Lack began. He drew his fist back, opened it up. The ring was still there.

"He doesn't like Professor Alice, and he doesn't like my wedding ring," he said. "But, watch." He picked up a strawberry, closed it in his fist, and repeated the demonstration. When he drew his hand back and opened it the strawberry was gone.

"Me and Lack, we have the same taste in dessert. Hah! It's a good magic show, but I keep the rest for myself." He popped a strawberry into his mouth, then twisted away the stem and laid it on a corner of the wax paper.

Lack doesn't like marriage, I thought. Alice and I should have gotten married. That was our mistake. Lack would have left us alone.

"It is very interesting, this idea your Professor Coombs has. Or is it more of an emotion than an idea, eh? I think so. To put herself into the Lack. You think it's terrible, I can see. But myself, I understand it a little. I feel it in myself too." He met my eyes. "You wish I didn't know about this idea of hers."

Humbled, I nodded.

"Here." He gestured at his sandwich. "You want some? Hen salad."

"Hen salad?"

"I'm losing a word. Rooster?"

"Rooster salad," I said. "No thank you."

He shrugged, took another bite of sandwich, and chewed it into one cheek. "You seem afraid that I am going to make some trouble for Professor Alice, eh? But you are wrong. I think it's charming. I want to help her."

"How?" I was jealous. "Help her disappear?"

Braxia swallowed the cheekful. "You know the outcome of the experiments," he said.

"Yes."

"The Lack never changes his mind. If he refuses something once, he refuses it forever. He is consistent in this way, yes?"

I nodded, feeling thick.

Braxia put down his sandwich and extended his arm through Lack again. "He will never take my ring, and he will never take Professor Alice. No matter what her passion dictates. No matter how often she tries. So it might be better, if she needs to try, that we let her. Yes?" He pulled his arm back. "Have a strawberry."

The barbed wire loosened from around my heart. "You really think he'll never take her?" I said.

"I really think he'll never take her," said Braxia, through another mouthful of sandwich.

"Would he take someone else?"

"I don't know, my dear fellow. It is a good question, but hard to ask, don't you think? Not too many volunteers. Strap on a transmitter, jump across the table. Hah!"

"Where would they end up? What's on the other side?"

"That's the whole question, isn't it? That's what we all want to know. Is it a tiny little universe in there? Maybe every time I drop a strawberry I crush three or four little suns! But who knows. We're trying." He indicated the roomful of equipment, with obvious pride. "When I have my answer, be sure, my dear fellow, you'll hear about it."

"You're sure it'll be you who gets the answer."

"Hah! Very good. Yes, I think so. Soft, he's not so strong anymore. He's in retreat. And your Professor Coombs, she's asking a very different kind of question now, I think. More about herself than about the Lack."

"What about the graduate students?"

"The graduate students." Braxia snorted. "Yes. Have you heard their proposal?"

"No."

"The idea is to build a monitor, an information-gathering device, out of only those materials the Lack desires. A Lack-compatible device, to launch across the table. Hah!" He slapped at Lack's table again. "It is very clever, and also deeply idiotic. Lack will refuse the device. You know why? They will build it out of driftwood, strawberries, whatever Lack likes. Then one day Lack changes his mind, says no more strawberries. Besides, the Lack likes things for themselves, not for components. A device is no longer the things it is made up of, it is a device. The students will be very lucky if Lack eats their monitor. No, they are in no danger of learning anything." He poked me in the chest. "If you were a physicist, perhaps you would be my competition. But."

"You seem to be saying that Lack is a metaphysical phenomenon. So I should be just as qualified as you to uncover his meaning. If he is, as you say, interested in the idea of things in themselves. Meanings. Texts."

Braxia's eyes bugged with excitement, as if he might inflate and float to the ceiling. Instead he seized up the final corner of his sandwich and pushed it into his mouth.

"Okay," he said. "Very good again. I like talking with you. Yes, Lack is interested in the idea, but not metaphysical. There is nothing metaphysical. We only have to uncover the underlying physics behind it. Soft created an experiment, remember? He wanted to do some fancy physics, bring something new into the world. And he succeeded. Hah! So now we take a good look at this thing. Texts, yes. That's a good word, texts. Soft has written a new text. But it is a physics text. From physics comes physics. I will prove it to you personally."

"I look forward to it."

"Oh, but don't stop your own work. I won't hear of it. Please, come and decode the text in your own way. I will follow your work eagerly. And while you read the book, I will tell you how and why there is a book, and more. I will tell you how there is a shelf for the book, and a house for the shelf, and so on."

"I'm sorry," I said. "I don't quite follow you."

"Listen, my dear fellow. I'm studying the universe. Lack is just a part, a clue. I'll explain Lack, and then I'll explain the rest to you, too. The whole thing. That's my job."

"So you're getting somewhere. You're learning something about Lack."

He screwed up his forehead. "I'll tell you something, Mr. Engstrand. I have twelve men here, young, headstrong ones, who can think of nothing but physics. Like Soft, or me, ten years ago. They do what I tell them, they work around the clock for me. We will shoot the Lack with sonar, radioactivity, demagnetized particles, tachyons, whatever I can cook up. I am very patient, Mr. Engstrand. I am going to find the signal that can bounce back out, and then I am going to describe the world to which the Lack is a door. Trust me, my dear fellow."

"But there's nothing yet."

"Just strawberries."

"And in the meantime you'll tolerate Alice, you'll tolerate me if I try, you'll tolerate doddering old Soft."

Braxia seemed entertained. "Yes," he said. "Certainly. I am fond of you already. Take your hours. I welcome you. You think I want to be here all day and all night? No! This weekend I am going to Sonoma."

"It's lovely."

"Yes. Besides, I will want you around to see when I have my breakthrough. You can document my discovery."

"Okay," I said. "You make a discovery. I'll document." I'd had enough of his bombast now. I turned to leave. Let Braxia and Lack enjoy their strawberries. Somewhere outside the sun was shining, somewhere skies were clear.

Before I got to the door of the chamber, though, he called to me.

109

"I forgot to tell you," he said. "When she came out of the chamber, she had her shirt on, what is the word? *Inside out.*" His eyes bored into mine, looking for reaction.

I refused to show one.

"Alice is your lady, eh?"

"Yes, Braxia. Alice is my lady. Or was."

"You know what? By solving Lack I will cure your Alice for you, give you her back."

"I hope so," I said honestly.

23

After her second refusal by Lack, Alice fled to her parents, an hour north, for Thanksgiving. From the horn of emptiness to the horn of plenty. I came home to find her stuffing underwear into a weekend suitcase, Evan and Garth standing stiffly to one side, canes lifted. She left without once meeting my eye. The blind men and I stood listening as her car, improperly warmed up, roared out of the driveway.

"Huh," said Garth, with deep sourness.

It rained that weekend. Evan and Garth and I went for walks in the mist. Weather seemed to lull the blind men to silence. It provided proof of an environment, so they no longer had to conjure one up by inventory. Turning their wet faces upward, losing shoes in the sucking mud of campus paths, they were finally convinced that their verbal weather was redundant, that a world loomed out around them.

111

I was thinking of Braxia's assurances. If it was true that Lack would never take Alice, then my struggle with Lack wasn't for her body, but for her mind, her soul. It was a struggle I felt I had a chance of winning. I sorted through long arguments in favor of myself, and against Lack. I measured my love for Alice against hers for Lack—which was craftier, which more tenacious? I was sure I knew the answer.

I'd woo her back.

On Thanksgiving I drove Evan and Garth to a dinner at the blind school, a large flat factory-like building in the middle of a grassy compound, surrounded by a baseball diamond, a parking lot, and a shallow blue swimming pool, drained for the winter and filling with dry leaves and the husks of summer insects. They invited me in, but I refused. I spent the afternoon driving in the hills above the city, nearly the only car, my radio tuned to live coverage of a far-off parade, athletes and politicians greeting crowds from garish floats. When it got dark I drove to my favorite diner, the Silver Lining, but the doors were closed. I peered in through the window. The vast, incomprehensible Greek family that ran the place was just sitting down to a pilgrim feast at the largest booth. The turkey was huge, golden, classic, and the side dishes were endless.

When I got back to the apartment I found—surprise!—Alice clearing out the bedroom to create a painting studio.

Alice was a terrible amateur painter. Or had been. At the start of our relationship she'd given it up. But now her dusty equipment was resurrected from the tomb of her parents' garage. Paint-splattered easel, drop cloths, and containers of gesso and rabbit-skin glue. A thick, square mirror, edges taped. The bookshelves had been moved into the living room, to expose the north wall. A roll of fresh white duck was leaning up against the door frame, blocking the entrance. Alice was in the kitchen, rinsing old brushes at the tap.

"Alice. You're back."

Silence.

"You missed the rest of your shift. Soft took over. I guess you'll have to wait until next week."

Silence. Water running in the sink.

I took a deep breath, trying to relocate my newfound, rain-washed strength.

"Possibly there's been a change," I suggested. "You're not so sure about this thing after all. You might be in over your head. Maybe you want to take a step back, get some perspective on this Lack thing."

Stony silence.

"Alice?" I moved up closer behind her. She went on gently kneading the encrusted bristles back to life.

"Maybe you're still in love with Lack," I said. "But feeling like you came on too strong. You're giving him some space, so he can mull it over."

Silence. I felt my schemes evaporating in it.

"Probably you're still in love with Lack," I said. "You're determined, nothing's going to stop you. You're going to try to change yourself for him. That's why you're painting again all of a sudden."

She shook a handful of brushes dry, and gathered them in a coffee can.

"Listen," I said. "I'm going to change my approach. I'm going to be lighthearted from here on in. We'll develop a lighthearted, bantering dialogue. Like an old movie. Like in *His Girl Friday*, when Cary Grant and Rosalind Russell are old flames, but she's going to marry somebody else. He stays lighthearted. They banter. But at the same time, he's making a very sly, very persuasive pitch for himself."

Silence.

"Or if you don't want to banter you could be like James Stewart in *Vertigo*, after he loses Kim Novak, the first time, and goes into a catatonic depression, and Barbara Bel Geddes has to try to jolly him out of it. With lighthearted banter. Because sometimes it's just one person carrying on the lighthearted banter and the other person listening. That's okay too."

I followed her into the bedroom, both of us ducking under the roll of canvas.

"I get it. You're not saying anything. Not a word. Why, I'll bet you haven't said a word since I came in here."

She began unrolling the canvas.

"I notice the mirror," I said. "I think I understand, I think I get it. You're going to paint self-portraits again. And offer them to Lack. Get him used to you, in stages. Is that the idea? It's very clever. If you hadn't thought of it before now you can give me the credit."

Silence.

"I get it. You're making yourself more like Lack by not talking, right?"

Silence that would seem to be confirmation.

"Okay. There's just one thing I want you to know, one thing I want to say. This is hardly lighthearted banter, I realize, but I just want to slip this in at the very start, and then I'll run with the banter from now on. I love you, Alice. It's important you hear that, it's important you know."

The silence was like a carcass in the room with us. A rotting defrosted mammoth of silence. Outside I heard a car door slam, and blind footsteps tapping their way up the porch stairs. Alice began chopping at the canvas with the scissors, her face beet red.

"I'm learning to hate the sound of my own voice," I said.

"I'm here as a patient," I said. I wanted roles to be clear.

Cynthia Jalter's daytime offices were in a private medical building in a sunny, modern complex near downtown Beauchamp. She shared a receptionist, waiting area, and piped-in Muzak selections with a Dr. Gavin Flapcloth. The office was even more generic than the informal counseling area in her apartment. The curtains, lamp shades, tissues, and the color in the sky of the small landscape in oils above the desk were all the same color, a meek, inoffensive yellow. It probably bore the name *buff* or *cockle*. The office had no windows. It was like being submerged in a glass of lukewarm eggnog.

Cynthia Jalter, on the other hand, was poised and elegant. Her black hair was swept back to expose her eyebrows, which met over her nose. She was the least blond woman I had ever met.

"I couldn't possibly take you on," she said. "We have a relationship outside this office."

"I'll relinquish that," I said. "I want you to dissect me. Understand my life."

She smiled. "We can't go backward. It doesn't work that way."

"My problems are couple related," I said. "I'm asking the advice of an expert."

"We met in a bar, you and I. You bought me a drink."

"That was fieldwork," I said. "You wanted to see me exhibit my tropism, my need to couple. Let's call it Life-Scenario Therapy."

"Two lonely people meeting in a bar."

My eyes wandered to a picture on the far wall. A faded print of a familiar painting: Brueghel's *Icarus,* falling into the ocean unseen.

"I need your help," I said. "Things you said have been haunting me. Delusory or subjective worlds. Dual cognitive systems. Inequal growth. Do they apply to me? I need to understand."

She sighed. "With what goal? Reentry? My understanding was that you're currently uncoupled."

"Am I? See, you've helped me already. That's exactly what I'm missing, a terminology to apply to my situation. Uncoupled. Of course. Cynthia, can't you see I'm operating at a disadvantage? Everyone around has a theory or an obsession. I'm making it up as I go along."

Cynthia Jalter lowered her head and smiled to herself. She set her clipboard on the desk and crossed her legs.

"You've got yourself mixed up with Alice's experiment,"

she said. "Lack's the one without any method. You're just using that as a cover."

"What are you saying?"

"You say you want my help, but I think you're kidding yourself. You want to avoid seeing the effect you're having on someone else. To avoid responsibility."

I stared blankly. The Muzak swelled.

"Do you know what I thought when you called?"

I was mute, wheels turning silently inside.

"I have to be honest with you, Philip. I'm not interested in your coming to me with problems about Alice. I don't think you have any. She's gone. What I would be interested in is seeing you exhibit your tropism."

I felt my face flush, my palms moisten. A common panic associated with frank avowals by dauntingly attractive women.

"I don't want to be your therapist," she said. "I might like to make love to you."

She leaned back in her chair. Her cheeks were a little flushed too. I felt courted, dizzy. Was it this simple? No more Alice? Could Cynthia Jalter simply uncouple me like a jigsaw-puzzle section and move me into her frame?

When I examined myself for response, I found a void, a lack.

"Is this an abuse of therapeutic confidence?" I said, dodging. "Can I lodge a complaint? Have I got a lawsuit?"

"I haven't accepted payment or even verbally contracted to see you professionally," she said. "We're just squatters in this office right now, not therapist and patient."

"Okay. No hard feelings. I just wanted to know."

"I understand. Besides, this might all be just some advanced therapeutic format. What did you call it? Life-Scenario Therapy."

I smiled weakly, at a loss. Cynthia Jalter got out of her seat, moved around her desk and out of view, then reappeared behind my chair, her arms draped over the back, her fingertips lightly touching my shoulders.

"Relax," she said.

"I am relaxed. It's just buried under layers of incredulity and panic. But underneath those I'm very relaxed."

"Philip."

"Also I am attracted to you. But I don't know how to approach a woman whose area of expertise is what goes wrong when people overlap."

"Don't worry."

"Also your office is like the living quarters of a space capsule they would use to send television talk-show hosts to other worlds."

"Should we go for a walk?"

"Yes."

She had a word with the receptionist, then we stepped outside, into the cold, sunny afternoon. She took my hand and led me around the corner, to a grassy courtyard behind the medical offices, sheltered from the street by a low brick wall. From there I could see the parking lot of the Look 'n' Like, the milling shoppers examining wreaths of pinecone and fir under a yellow tarpaulin. I looked up and caught a blurry figure moving behind the pebbled glass of the medical building windows.

I pointed. "Dr. Flapcloth?"

Cynthia Jalter nodded.

"Another couple therapist?"

"Vagina ecologist."

"What?"

She repeated it.

"You mean a gynecologist."

"Yes and no. Gavin prefers to break it into the root words to capture a meaning he feels is lost. The ecology of the vagina, the vagina as environment, rather than just negative space."

"And himself as what? E.P.A. official?"

Cynthia Jalter laughed. The wind blew a strand of black hair into her mouth, and she ran it back out with a finger.

I thought of Lack as cosmic vagina, laid out across that cold steel table for examination. Unable to close his legs. Peered into by dozens of white-coated experts. Maybe Alice just wanted to shelter this vaginal entity.

Cynthia Jalter squeezed my hand. She blinked as the wind whipped her hair across her face. "You don't have to stay with Alice anymore," she said, apparently reading my thoughts. "You've been patient enough. It's not your fault. You're free now to do anything you want."

Though it was cold, a layer of moisture was forming between our clenched hands.

"What if I want to stay with Alice?" I said.

She smiled. "Just don't forget that there are other options. That your life can change. People do forget." She tugged my hand and drew me close enough to kiss. Her lips were dry and cool. I thought I could feel her smiling around my mouth.

It only lasted an instant. Just long enough for me to wonder if I was numb to Cynthia Jalter the way Alice was numb to me, the way Lack was numb to Alice. Were we links in a chain?

More important, if I woke to Cynthia Jalter, entered her embrace, would that start a chain reaction—would Lack embrace Alice?

The kiss was over before I could puzzle it out. Our lips stuck together slightly as we separated. Whatever else, I'd have a small secret now. This kiss would be with me, invisible badge or scar, when I went back to the apartment.

I opened my eyes. A tiny plane droned overhead, low against the fluffy clouds, trailing a banner that read CELESTE WILL YOU MARRY ME MAYNARD. A simple message conveyed across vast distance. Admirable. The answer could only be yes. The plane circled the patch of sky above the courtyard, then vanished.

I looked at Cynthia Jalter.

"I need time to think," I said. "I'm living with two men who can't see and a woman who won't talk. She's painting self-portraits now. She only eats toast. It's tempting to think I can just walk away, but I can't. Lack is part of my life at this point. I have to see it through to the end. I'm as bound to it as Alice."

Cynthia Jalter took me by the shoulder and kissed me again, quickly, almost furtively, on the corner of my mouth. I was left puckering in the cold air, late.

"I understand," she said. She seemed confident.

What did she know that I didn't?

"Relax," she said. "There's nothing wrong with a slow, awkward beginning. The text for the whole relationship, the sustaining mythos, is built in the first few encounters. The whirl of emotions, the push and pull. So the more of this kind of material we generate, the better."

I couldn't speak.

"We're sitting pretty," she said.

My knees were locked. I had no voice. A tendril of her hair floated loose and swept against my cheek. I tucked it back behind her ear, and came awfully close to grabbing her and kissing her again. But the impulse tangled into knots. Instead I raised my hand and pointed to the parking lot, indicating my small brown Datsun.

"You have to go," she said.

I made a steering wheel shape with my hands.

25

Georges De Tooth was our resident deconstructionist, a tiny, horse-faced man who dressed in impeccable pinstriped suits, spoke in a feigned poly-European accent, and wore an overlarge, ill-fitting, white-blond wig. He could be seen hurrying between the English department and his car, an enormous leather briefcase gripped in both arms as if it were the cover of a manhole from which he had just emerged. Or sitting in faculty meetings, silent and pensive, chewing on the stem of an unloaded pipe, often held with the bowl facing sideways or down. The library housed a dozen or so of his slim, unreadable volumes, as well as a thick anthology of savage attacks by his enemies. He lived in a room at the YMCA. He had for fifteen years.

When I ushered De Tooth into Soft's office it was, as far as I knew, the first meeting between the two great men. It wasn't auspicious. They clutched quickly at each other's hands, mumbled in unison, and retreated together into silence. I offered De Tooth a seat and he took it, trapping himself underneath his briefcase, his nose and wig peeking out over the top, his feet dangling above the floor. Soft leaned back in his chair, caught my eye, and screwed up his eyebrows in a frown. I smiled back.

De Tooth was my version of Braxia. The European surrogate, the trump card. I'd spent the past week wooing him, baiting his interest in Lack. When I captured it I began priming him for this encounter. This was my own particle collision, my chance to bump together incompatible fields. Now I would observe the event.

"Professor De Tooth and I have conceived an approach to Lack," I said. "As I said on the phone, I wanted to run it by you. Otherwise we're all ready to go. We just need some lab time."

"You know you have my support, Philip. You know I want to see you in there."

"Yes, well. We're proposing something unorthodox, but very exciting. It's not as though we'll be in the way of the other teams. There shouldn't be any problem."

"Unorthodox."

"Yes." I turned to look at De Tooth. He'd slid the briefcase to his knees, though he still gripped the handle with both hands. He was studying Soft. "A contemporary critical approach," I went on. "Very fertile. We want to treat Lack as a self-contained text. A sign. We want to read him."

Soft paled slightly.

"In this field we speak of the text, in this case Lack, as possessing an independent life, free of context," I went on. "We derive our descriptive standards, our critical vocabulary, from the source. Lack again. The idea is that any given text contains its own decryption kit, if we approach it free of bias."

"Interesting," said Soft. He closed his eyes.

"Have you heard," said De Tooth, "of the death of the author?" When he spoke he arched his eyebrows, and they disappeared into the yellow wig.

Soft looked at De Tooth. I could practically see the interference pattern in the space between the two men. The bad splice.

"I may have," said Soft.

"It's quite simple," said De Tooth. "We admit the presence of no author, no oeuvre, and no genre. The text stands bare. We discard biography, psychology, historicism—these things impede clear vision. We admit nothing outside of the text. Lack is no different. In his case the irrelevant genre is physics, and the irrelevant author is yourself. We will study Lack as if he authored himself."

Soft smiled weakly. "Your study consisting of what?"

"More text," said De Tooth. "The only possible response."

"Georges will create a corresponding artifact," I explained. "The correct approach to a text as dense and self-consistent and original as Lack is a criticism with all the same qualities."

"You mean you'll sit in the chamber and write?" Soft sounded uncomfortable.

De Tooth shrugged. "In or out of the chamber, I will compose a document. Perhaps it will not mention Lack. Perhaps it will only consist of the word *Lack*. And my students, in turn, will study my text. Without access to Lack. We should use up a minimum of your precious time."

"With all due respect," said Soft, "Lack isn't exactly a work of art."

"Leave that to me to determine. Meaning accrues in unexpected places. And drains unexpectedly out of others. Your physics, for example, has proven insufficient."

125

I had a sudden inspiration. "Maybe we can offer the new text to Lack, to see if he'll take it in."

"Lack *is* physics," protested Soft feebly. "You can't separate the two."

"Lack, Mr. Soft, is a singular monument transcending any banal explanation. Lack has a prodigious propensity to meaning. He seems to attract it like a lightning rod. For a lover of signification like myself, an irresistible phenomenon. Pure signifier. Lack is a verb both active and passive; an object and a space at once, a symbol. He is no single thing. Physics seeks to dismantle the surface, perceive beyond it, to a truth comprised of particles; I argue against depth wherever I find it. Lack's meaning is all on the surface, and his surface appears to be infinite. Your approach is useless."

De Tooth rattled on, his distended lips forming the brittle sentences. Soft withered, and turned pea yellow. I started to feel protective. I wanted to hurry De Tooth away. The point had been made. But the little man, his tiny knuckles clenched white on the handle of his briefcase, was unstoppable.

"Perhaps my text and yours will cancel each other out. They so often do, you know. It is possible Lack is no more than an assertion that has gone, until now, unanswered. Or perhaps Lack is a tool, a method, whose use has so far remained undiscovered. Certainly, in fact, Lack is all of these, and more. Lack is the inevitable: the virtually empty sign. The sign that means everything it is possible to mean, to any reader."

Soft put his hand against his pale, sticky forehead. "Does it seem a little warm in here?"

There was no reply. Soft tugged at the knot of his tie. "Go on," he said finally. "I didn't mean to interrupt."

"Perhaps we shall prove that Lack does not exist," said De

Tooth. Soft looked at me plaintively from beneath his hand. "And perhaps we shall prove that we ourselves do not exist. Perhaps Lack is editing the world for us, sorting it into those things that truly exist and those that do not; we who fail to exist may only peer with nostalgia across the threshold into reality; we may not cross."

Soft got out of his seat and went to the open window. He was breathing through his mouth.

"Are you okay?" I said.

Soft shook his head.

I got up and took him by the shoulder, and guided him through the door and into the hallway, where he slumped against the wall. He slid his hand from his panic-stricken eyes and used it to cover his mouth. His face had turned a brackish green. De Tooth hopped off his chair and dragged his briefcase out to where we stood in the hall.

"Perhaps Lack has dreamed us, and we are only now, due to some scientific blunder, encountering the mind's eye of our dreamer."

Soft choked and doubled up, pencils spilling from his shirt pocket and scattering on the floor. When he straightened there was spittle hanging from between his fingers. "I'm sorry," he gasped. He hobbled down the hall, into the men's room. I heard a retching sound echoing faintly off the tile.

I looked at De Tooth. He arched his eyebrows into his wig.

Three nights later, Alice loaded up the back of her Toyota with fifteen or twenty dashed-off paintings, and drove the short distance to the physics facility. She parked in the faculty lot, then piled the paintings through the main entrance and into the elevator.

I followed at a safe distance in my Datsun, and then on foot. Unseen.

The canvases were mostly self-portraits, painted in nervous, choppy brush strokes, images hacked out of the murk. There were a few abstractions, and a few still lifes. One painting of Evan and Garth. I liked her new work, actually. It was better than the earlier stuff. Maybe the emotional strain had freed her inhibitions, pushed her closer to the edge where art occurs. She'd certainly perfected a kind of 1950s painter's temperament: surly, nonverbal, and permanently strung out.

But would Lack like them?

We were going to find out.

When the elevator doors closed, I took the stairs, feeling like a spy. The stairwell, with its bare concrete walls, fallout-shelter notices, and unadorned light bulbs glaring from within iron cages, was perfect for espionage fantasies. It went on and on. There were three landings, three twists of stair, for every numbered floor. The building had extra depths, layers the elevator skipped. I wondered if the building contained its own opposite, an anti-building where anti-physicists collided anti-particles. Anti-men who paused only to wonder at the odd sounds coming from the floors and ceilings.

At Lack's floor I opened the emergency exit. I was alone in the corridor—no Alice. I went into the observation room and found Braxia, dressed in a lab coat, eating an apple, chewing with his mouth open.

He tilted his head to indicate the chamber. "She wants privacy," he said.

"She took the paintings in?"

He nodded.

So Alice was alone inside, with Lack. The fundamental situation. This was the closest I'd come to it. I was annoyed to have Braxia there.

"She's offering the paintings to Lack," I said. "They're self-portraits. Surrogate selves."

Braxia smiled, crunched, swallowed. "Is something like physics, I think. To paint a self-portrait. You look at this thing, and it moves. You try to portray it, and it changes. You look out of the corner of your eye, it eludes you. You stare straight, you widen your eyes, and it makes a face at you."

129

I slumped down against the wall, across from the entrance to the chamber, fixing my gaze on Braxia's kneecaps.

"Okay," he said. "You can't talk now, about interesting things. You have to be worried and serious. I understand. So, if you will stay and be worried, I will go home and take a nap. You think I want to stay down here all night? I'll watch television."

"I'll stay," I said.

"It could be a long time," he said. "You want to get some dinner, come back? I'll wait."

"I'm fine."

Braxia shrugged, and went out. A moment later I heard the gurgle of the elevator as it ferried him up to the lobby.

Leaving me alone, on AliceWatch.

I stretched out my legs, checked the time, took a deep breath. This was what I wanted, supposedly, to have her under my care. So I settled down to wait.

I started by listening intently, then realized there was nothing to hear.

I tensed my body for action. Then untensed it. There wasn't any action.

My brain composed another bright dialogue. But I knew Alice wouldn't provide the responses needed to cue my witticisms.

Alice was alone with her Lack. I was alone with mine. Mine was less interesting than hers, I realized. She was obsessed, and I was bored. Bored and hungry and lonely.

I was lonely for anyone, lonely for a human voice. Cynthia Jalter, maybe. Or Evan and Garth. I was lonely enough to wish Braxia would come back and jabber at me.

The pay phone was just out of sight around the curve of the

hallway. I could order food. I'd only abandon Alice for a moment. I went to the phone. The directory had been half-shredded out of its protective binder, but I found the number of a pizzeria near campus.

"I want a small pizza and a bottle of beer," I explained to the boyish voice on the other end of the line. "But no cheese. Can you give me a small pizza without cheese?"

"That's unusual," said the voice. "Let me check. I'll put you on hold."

He came back. "One small pizza, no cheese. Any specials?"

"Specials?"

"Special aspects, you know. Things. Mushroom, garlic, pineapple."

"Mushrooms."

"Just one? You get a discount if you get three."

I thought about it. "What if we consider no cheese a special?"

"Um, okay. So let's see, that's one small pizza, mushrooms, no cheese. Pick one more."

"How about no pineapple?"

There was a pause. "Let me check."

"Forget it," I said when he came back. "I don't want a pizza. No cheese was the giveaway. Can you just bring me the beer? Talking about pizza made me thirsty."

"I don't think I can do that, sir. I think just beer is against the rules, and it might even be illegal. I might get fired or arrested."

"Check," I said. "Put me on hold."

"I think I'll do that, sir."

I heard footsteps in the corridor, moving toward the elevator. Startled, I dropped the phone, and ran to look. A woman was just disappearing around the curve. Alice's height, and blond, but with hair cut close to her scalp, in a ragged, amateur crew cut. Someone else, in other words. But where had she come from? I dashed back to the chamber, baffled.

The door was open. I looked inside. No Alice. The spotlight glared against Lack's bare table, creating a blinding reflection. The room was like a set for a Beckett play. A pair of scissors lay on the floor, and a stack of Alice's paintings leaned against the far wall. Otherwise the room was empty. I went to the paintings. They were the self-portraits, Alice's tortured menagerie of selves.

The other paintings were gone, the still lifes and abstractions, the painting of Evan and Garth. Lack had taken those.

He'd found her other work to his liking, apparently. But not the self-portraits.

Then I saw the yellow shadow scattered across the floor, beside the scissors. It was Alice's hair. Her blond hair. My pillow, once. I'd stained it with tears. Now it was on a lab floor. I reached down and gathered up a handful, and held it to my nose. Alice's smell. I remembered her brushing her hair, head lowered. I remembered yanking on it as we fucked. Here it was, hacked off, tossed at Lack, and refused. I dropped it and ran out into the hallway. She was gone.

27

"I was reading about the dark matter," said Evan.

We were sitting on a sunny patch of lawn in front of the library. The ground was cool and wet and the monolithic school buildings seemed like a distant hallucination. Evan was at my right, his legs folded underneath him, his head lolled onto one shoulder, like a schoolgirl. Garth, at my left, sat on his haunches like a baseball catcher, his tongue out, hands gripping fistfuls of the damp grass. At the other end of the field a marching band practiced making turns in step, their instruments, heavy tubas and kettledrums, all silent.

"The dark matter?" I said.

"Ninety percent of the matter in the universe is impossible to detect. But they know it's there. They need it to balance their equations. To hold up the other stuff."

133

Garth ripped out a tuft of grass, held it to his nose, wrinkled his brow.

"That's what it's like for us," Evan went on. "Everything is dark matter. We're always setting up experiments, trying to confirm the existence of the dark matter. But we can't. We just have to trust that it's there."

Garth picked up his cane, and used the tip to root in the earth.

"And then I was wondering," said Evan. "Maybe Garth and I are in the wrong universe. Maybe in some other universe there's a form of matter that's visible to us. Maybe if we were much smaller. Subatomic."

"Huh," said Garth suddenly. "I was supposed to see the particles. I didn't see anything."

Garth, characteristically, was trying to drag Evan out of talking to me, back into their neurotic loop. Evan hesitated. I could see he wanted to resist the gravitational pull of Garth's bitterness. But he was drawn by habit.

Garth stopped digging, and waited for a response, his nostrils flared.

"But we do see things," said Evan, to me. "We talk about it when we're alone. Retinal patterns. We see them all the time, you know. We can't close our eyes and stop. Maybe that's the dark matter. Maybe you see ten percent of reality, and Garth and I see ninety percent."

"Huh," said Garth.

"Cynthia calls them forms and colors," said Evan. "She says that's what we're seeing."

"You don't even know which one is a form and which one is a color," said Garth.

"I do too. Remember what Cynthia said: Forms are like sounds, and colors are like smells. So a red cloud, for instance, might be a certain sound combined with a certain smell."

"But you can't know. Cynthia can't see what you see."

Evan cleared his throat. "It doesn't matter."

"But you can't know," said Garth, pounding it home.

I hated Garth suddenly. He was a dead weight around the neck of the world. Around Evan's neck, anyway. Cynthia should pry them apart.

We fell silent. Evan sat dejectedly. Garth digged determinedly in the moist ground with his cane. I watched the winter clouds, and my thoughts drifted to Alice.

"What is see?" said Garth.

"What?" said Evan.

"What is see? What is see?"

The marching band approached us, still in formation, still miming their playing. Evan and Garth looked up and trained their ears on the disturbance. The band marched past us, the only sound their quiet synchronized tramping on the grass, and a soft clicking as the horn players opened and closed their valves.

"See is just a movie in your eyes," said Garth. "It's not out in the world."

"A movie?"

"It's not out there, it's not dark matter or anything else. It's just in your eyes. A movie. And the only difference is that everyone else has the same movie playing. Cynthia, Philip, Alice, their movies agree. So they can see. You and I are watching the wrong movie, so we're blind."

Evan and I were silent.

"See is a dream," said Garth. "There isn't anything to see. Real things come one at a time. They come into your hand, and then disappear. Huh.'' He felt at the end of his cane, then put his hand to his chin and left a smear of mud there. ''See is a movie. But when something goes wrong in their movie, when something is odd, they don't question themselves. They don't say, gee, things are disappearing in this laboratory, something must be wrong with my eyes or my brain, I must be blind. They put it outside of themselves, they say, gee, something is wrong with the *world*. There must be a Lack. Well, I say we're not blind anymore. I say something is wrong with the world. People talk about things that aren't there. And they never talk about what's in their hands.''

''But that's exactly what I was saying,'' said Evan.

''Exactly,'' said Garth.

''But you contradicted me.''

''But now you see I didn't.''

I looked at Evan. If he'd had eyes, he would have looked at me. We would have shared a knowing look, one that excluded Garth. But he couldn't enter my glance. I was the one excluded. Evan and Garth were alone together, in another world.

They belonged together, I thought now. Cynthia should help them to see that.

''Do you remember when I said I might be lying about the precise location of certain objects?'' said Garth.

''Yes,'' said Evan.

''Well, don't worry,'' said Garth. ''I don't know where they are either.''

28

I went back down the next day, to watch as the graduate group introduced their custom-built probe to Lack. The faculty heavy-weights were all present: Braxia, Soft, De Tooth, myself. All except Alice. The fresh-faced graduate students set up their experiment around us, taping cables and cords to the floor, testing transmitters and recording devices. At the last minute they unveiled their probe.

At first I thought it was too big for Lack. But they had his measurements, based on the particle screen hits, and this thing must have been made to fit. It resembled a cube of compacted garbage, or an assignment by an eccentric art teacher. Construct an interplanetary probe exclusively from the following list of materials: first baseman's mitt, two-dollar bill, French horn, salad spinner, cotton swab. It had treads for negotiating terrain, like a moon buggy, a robot arm for righting itself or seizing objects, and dishes and antennae pointed in every direction, hoping for a signal.

137

They brought it in on its own steel table. It was like a reply to Lack, a presence to equal the absence, a Frankenstein's Monster to master the Invisible Man. I could hear a fan inside, humming ominously. The students pushed the table up to Lack's and then backed away. They seemed a little awed by their own hurried, patchwork creation.

Soft looked the most optimistic. These were his students, after all. A triumph for them would vindicate the department. He stood closest, on the fringe of the students, hovering like an older brother. Braxia, on the other hand, stood to one side, his crossed arms and sour expression underlining his prediction of failure. This was not only a waste of Lack-time, his expression seemed to say, but a personal affront, an abuse of precious Braxia-hours.

And then there was De Tooth. What a roomful of Frankensteins, I thought, with our monsters all in attendance! Soft had Lack and Braxia, the students had their ungainly probe, and I had De Tooth. The deconstructionist had undone his briefcase, and papers were spilled out all around him. He scribbled frantically into a pad propped awkwardly on his knees, pausing only to cast accusatory glances in every direction. Two days before I'd received a letter from him, a manifesto, declaring his independence from me in his work with Lack, decrying my status as "false auteur." He'd insisted on a complete blackout of communication between us. When he caught my eye now he scowled, then crumpled the page in his lap and tossed it aside, as if it had been polluted by my gaze.

Alice was Frankenstein *and* Monster, I supposed. Creator first, in that vibrant period when she'd seized Soft's project away. Now, mute, tormented, and crew-cut, she was a monster. And Lack was her creator.

After interminable spot checks, test signals, and huddled

conferences, the team abandoned the paired tables, leaving their machine alone to face its invisible twin. There was a modest countdown, and the device began to crawl on its treads toward Lack, to attempt to carry off the incestuous union. I was horrified. Wasn't the device as much of a scientific aberration as Lack? They were definitely siblings. They might as well use Lack to investigate the mystery of the probe.

The object wobbled perilously at the joint of the two tables. We held our breath. Then a foot descended from the interior of the probe, to steady it, and the treads reengaged. The machine rolled on. We breathed again. The students stood ready to receive signals from the other side, from inside Lack, or beyond Lack, whichever it was. From un-Lack. We all stared as the probe lumbered up to Lack's entrance. Hoping, despite ourselves. Even Braxia, I imagine. We forgave it existing long after it really should have disappeared.

Soon, though, it was unmistakably past Lack, and still in awkward grinding evidence on the table. For that moment when it drove on toward the far edge it seemed full of misguided valor, an object of beauty, a Quixote in full armor, but as its treads jutted idiotically over the rim of the table, and especially once it plopped stupidly off the end to crash in a heap on the tiles, treads spinning hopelessly in the air, arm fighting loose of the wreckage to grope hopelessly for orientation, it was only an embarrassment. The students turned from their monitors, clicked off their instruments, hitched their thumbs in the belt loops of their corduroys or adjusted their eyeglasses, but nobody approached the wreck. Soft coughed. Braxia rubbed at his chin. De Tooth went on scribbling. I left.

29

The next night I found Alice alone in the apartment. The blind men were at Cynthia Jalter's. Alice was sitting cross-legged in the middle of the bed, drawing in a spiral-bound notebook. She'd cleaned up the painting supplies. The lamp by the bed was the only light on in the apartment. Alice's boyish, lopsided haircut had been growing out its worst irregularities, and I found myself actually charmed by the androgynous curve of her neck and scalp.

The apartment was quiet. We were quiet. I stood in the doorway and she looked up at me. If I didn't talk, her silence wasn't anything abnormal. Maybe we were about to touch. As I recalled that kind of mutual, affectionate silence I stared, and she stared back.

My inner chemistry had been hijacked by a mad scientist, who poured the fizzy, volatile contents of my heart from a test tube marked SOBER REALITY into another labeled SUNNY DELUSION, and back again, faster and faster, until the floor of my life was slick with spillage.

"Do you want some coffee?" I said.

She stared.

"I guess that's a bit naive, thinking you'll break your silence to ask for coffee. Anyway, you probably just had coffee, just now."

She continued to stare.

"Tea?" I said. "We could have tea. I heard someone say tea builds bridges between people. Coffee is more isolationist."

Alice smiled. My head flushed with blood.

"I'll make tea, then. I'll go out and get some. You stay there. Keep smiling."

"Philip," she said.

"You spoke."

"Stop talking," she said. "Stop for a minute."

I nodded, which she missed.

"Why do you keep trying to talk to me, Philip?"

"That's it? You open your mouth to ask me why I talk to you? That's what you have to say?"

She nodded.

The mad scientist dumped both test tubes on the floor, and the contents ran down the drain marked EMBITTERED.

"I've thought about shutting up, believe it or not. But I think the solution is more talk, not less. I could learn ventriloquism. Ask questions and answer them myself. After Evan and Garth move out we could get some cats and dogs, and I could make up funny voices for them."

No reaction.

"I talk to offer some contrast to Lack, to help you understand your options. I talk, he doesn't. I talk because I've been consulting with an expert in ontological breakdown and he prescribes inane chatter. Doctor's orders. You think I like this? It's a living nightmare. I hear my voice in dreams, offering you coffee. This is a bedside vigil, an act of faith. And now the patient rouses to ask if I would please pull the plug on the respirator."

I heard footsteps. And cane taps, outside. A car door slamming. The blind men were back.

"I talk because—listen, before they get inside, let me ask you a question: Do you think Garth would make a good blues singer? Or is that racist? I'm thinking of buying him a guitar for Christmas. You can write your answer down on a piece of paper."

The blind men clattered through the front door, into the darkened apartment. Alice looked away from me. Garth buzzed straight through to the kitchen, to the humming refrigerator, which spilled light into the living room. Evan walked a tight circle at the doorway until he stood facing me, approximately.

"Philip?" he said. "Cynthia wants to talk to you. She's waiting outside."

I looked at Alice again. Her eyes were stony. The moment of connection was over. If it had happened at all. Perhaps "Alice," as previously formulated, resided more in my memory than in the depleted original container.

"Stay there," I said to her. "We'll talk more in a minute. Practice moving your lips and tongue while I'm gone."

A car horn tooted. I went out. Cynthia sat waiting inside her rumbling, steaming Pontiac. I went to the passenger window. She powered it down a crack from her place behind the wheel. "Get in," she said.

I slid in beside her. "Are you with the mob?"

"Close the door."

She rolled up the window and clicked on the overhead light. Our breath fogged the windows. Seated, her long legs tucked under the dash, Cynthia Jalter was the same size as me. The car was spacious, but I still felt huddled in a tiny place with her, like titillated children playing in a cardboard box.

She dug for something in her purse. "Here." She appeared with a thin, hand-rolled cigarette in her mouth, a lighter in her hand.

"What's that?"

"Drugs," she said, muffled through pressed-together lips. She ignited the cigarette. The surplus paper flared, then died, and the tip pulsed orange.

"Don't set your hair on fire. I've forgotten how to smother the flames of a burning woman inside a car. What's that called, the Leibnitz Maneuver? Anyway, I've forgotten it."

"Come here," she said, squeezing the words out airlessly. She crooked her finger and bugged her eyes.

"I am here. You know, I have to go back inside in a minute and carry on both ends of a very important conversation—"

Cynthia Jalter put her hand behind my neck, caught my mouth in an open, passionate kiss, and blew a lungful of smoke down my throat. I gulped, swallowing some of it, rerouting a measure through my nose, and inhaling the rest.

"You're not going back in there," she said. "You're coming with me." She wiped a porthole in the foggy windshield, and shifted the car out of neutral.

I spewed my smoke into the tiny airspace of the car, filling it completely. "You are with the mob, I knew it. This is a hit."

"Yes."

"I don't have my coat." I hiccupped out more smoke.

"You'll be fine." She steered us out of my driveway, meanwhile drawing on the joint again, then passing it to me. I inhaled a smaller, more manageable portion. My head was already swimming, probably just from holding my breath. As I puffed inexpertly, the sealed space of the car continued to fill with smoke, becoming a kind of iron lung.

"Where are we going?"

"To my office. Give me that." She smoked aggressively, her eyes on the road. "Take this." She handed it back.

"Why are we smoking this?" I asked between breaths.

"To relax."

"Why do we want to relax?"

She didn't answer. We pulled up outside her office and got out in what must have appeared to be a minor explosion of smoke. The streets of Beauchamp were oddly quiet. Cynthia Jalter unlocked the door and we went in.

When she switched on the lights the Muzak appeared too, surprisingly loud. I noticed how intricate and well-played it was. Cynthia Jalter unlocked her office and drew me inside.

"Wait," I said. "Listen to this."

"I'm sorry. I don't know how to turn it off."

"It's beautiful."

She smiled. "Come with me."

"Actual people played this music with actual instruments at some actual time," I said. "Think of that. Actual musicians actually playing. In a recording studio. With ashtrays and cups of coffee, probably. They must have done dozens of takes sometimes. This might be take six on this particular tune. The keeper."

"They probably always get it right the first time."

"Do you think there are bootleg tapes of Muzak outtakes?

Maybe they get excited by the groove and really cut loose sometimes. And the producer says, okay, boys, that was swell but now let's try to get this wrapped so we can all go home. I bet that happens all the time."

"In here," she said.

She shut the door behind us, sealing us into her dangerously plush office. I sat on the sofa. It reminded me of the Muzak, and they both reminded me, as before, of eggnog.

I craved eggnog.

Cynthia Jalter sat beside me on the sofa, turned in my direction, her legs crossed. I sat facing her desk, my hands in my lap. I realized she was staring at me and turned and looked. She smiled. She was radiantly beautiful. I felt a flush of gratitude that she had taken me away from my apartment and brought me to this wonderful place. I was glad she wasn't blond.

"Philip."

"Cynthia Jalter."

"You don't have to say Jalter."

"I like to. Why did we come to your office, Cynthia Jalter?"

"You're in a destructive relationship. I'm helping you. I'm your therapist."

"This is therapy?"

"Yes."

"It's very nice."

"You like it?" She smiled.

"Yes. Do you have any eggnog?"

"Eggnog?"

"Yes. The music sounds like eggnog. Do you know where we can get some? It's almost Christmastime."

"Maybe after therapy we'll go for eggnog."

"Therapy. Oh, yes."

Cynthia Jalter took my shoulder and turned me toward her, then drew her hair back and leaned forward. Her features were arranged in a special shape, a shape I recognized. She put her face against mine. A kiss. The sticky part of her face found mine, and they oscillated together.

Cynthia Jalter leaned back and sighed.

"I've never had this kind of therapy before," I said. "I'm more accustomed to the talking kind."

"You want to talk?"

I nodded. "Talk about couples. Coupling. The right and wrong way."

She sighed. "Well, the wrong way is like you and Alice. Circumscribed, myopic, inflexible. You formed a vulnerable mutual world-sphere."

"What?"

"The sphere ruptured at the slightest pressure."

"Oh," I said, bewildered. "What's the right way?"

"I'm going to show you the right way," she said. She aligned our faces again, and we kissed. I helped. She slipped inside the shelter of my arm, which lay across the back of the couch. I put my hand on the nape of her neck, and wove my fingers into her long, smooth hair. It felt black. My hand was swallowed in it. Like an object swallowed by Lack. No, I thought, I shouldn't be doing that, she wants me to stay separate. Don't merge. It's better not to merge.

Something entered my mouth. The texture was extraordinary. Tongue. I tried to provide it a toothless, serene environment there, in my mouth. It seemed to be looking for something. Of course. My tongue. Tongue wants other tongue.

Reports came in from other fronts. My right hand was exploring a softness and pleasantness that lacked an important name. Muzak? Eggnog? Breast. I felt a nipple, like a warm pebble in my palm. Then the softness swirled, became less definite. And the tongue, when I checked, was missing from my mouth. The extra tongue.

"Philip," Cynthia Jalter breathed into my ear.

"Therapist," I breathed back, except it came out an unintelligible croak.

She slid off the couch and onto the carpet, quite smoothly, and without letting go of me. So I began by watching her go, detached at least intellectually, and ended on the carpet with her, painlessly. The couch and the carpet seemed somehow continuous, like they were meant for this.

"Philip," she said again.

"Cynthia," I whispered. "Have you noticed that I'm croaking like a frog?"

"I hadn't noticed."

"Also this isn't therapy, I'm sure of it."

"That's okay."

"Also I'm having some trouble identifying various parts of your body. Maybe when I come into contact with something new you could just call out the name aloud."

"Is there numbness in your extremities?"

"Should there be? I think this is more a numbness in the female-anatomy-naming part of my brain. Also I'm thinking about Alice a little, I have to admit. And croaking like a frog, can you hear that?"

"I see what you mean but it's nothing very important. You could talk less. You talk a lot."

"Okay, but I am thinking about Alice a little bit, like I said."

Cynthia Jalter sighed, and shifted so that my hip slid to rest on the carpet.

"If you want to go on being in love with Alice," she said, "this therapy will help you do it in a more self-reliant way. I'll identify the various parts of my body if you like, and I can also talk about the various phases of the brief affair we're sharing, so you'll develop both vocabularies at the same time. But while we're on the subject I do want to say I think you're wasting your time pining after a woman who stopped giving you what you need months ago. And you might be ignoring a very interesting alternative."

"Ah."

"Now kiss me."

She didn't wait, but kissed me. Our bodies slid together so that they aligned in several crucial places, all of which had names that I would probably remember, or not. It didn't matter. My body knew how to answer all the questions hers was posing, was busy answering them, in fact, despite my reservations. I was turned on, happy even, sandwiched there with Cynthia between carpet and Muzak.

Something happened to my penis. Cynthia Jalter had hold of it, the end of it, and was kneading rhythmically, sending me signals. It was a message of some sort, on my private-access channel, my hot line, my Batphone. Maybe it was the secret of the universe. If the medium is the message, it was for sure. So I was about to learn the secret of the universe. I should be pleased.

I sat up.

"What's the matter?"

"Therapy is supposed to help you understand."

"Yes. Come back down here and I'll help you understand."

"I don't want to understand."

"You don't want to understand what, Philip?"

"My coupling with Alice. I just want it back. I can't stop wanting that."

Cynthia sighed. She tugged her twisted clothes back into place. "You don't want to make love to me."

"I'm sorry."

"It's okay. Should we go out and find you some eggnog? This could be the start of a friendship that only gradually unfolds to reveal mutual desire."

"Maybe you should drive me home. I don't feel good."

It was true. I felt like a mummy, shrouded in carpet and Muzak. I needed fresh air.

Cynthia Jalter buttoned her shirt. Had I unbuttoned it? Had she? Was it an advanced form of shirt that unbuttoned itself?

She led me outside, and I gulped at the night air, as I had the marijuana fumes. I wanted to reverse the damage, clear my brain. Cynthia Jalter went to her car and warmed the engine. I got in beside her. My head throbbed. We drove in silence back to campus.

"Don't worry," said Cynthia Jalter as we pulled up outside the apartment. "I understand. You don't have to say a word. Forget this ever happened, if you like. Or change your mind, come find me. I want you to feel okay about this."

"Okay."

"You're making the worst mistake of your life. I resent you for being so blind. You'd better win Alice back, and it had better be wonderful, because after this anything less is inexcusable."

"That doesn't go with the other thing you just said," I said.

"I know. You can choose which of them you prefer. I'm comfortable either way."

"Do I have to say now?"

"No, take your time, let me know later."

"Okay. Good night, Cynthia."

"Good night, Philip."

I went inside. The house was quiet, the blind men asleep. I crept in to look at Alice, in our old bed, where she was sleeping. She looked very peaceful. I got under the covers beside her, fully dressed. She stirred, but didn't wake. I curled around her and quickly fell asleep. When I awoke the next morning she was gone.

30

It was a week until Christmas. Two days until the end of the term. National Entropy Awareness Week, according to the papers. A cloud of stress hung over the campus. Students appeared in my office ranting or shaking like heretics. Tempera Santas appeared on store windows, and immediately began flaking into colorful drifts in the window displays underneath. Braxia announced that the Italian team would fly back to Pisa at the end of the term. They were abandoning Lack. My sports-injury student called me, badly shaken. His results had been published in an in-house journal of the Navy Seals, been taken as relevant to combat situations. On Tuesday hail fell, lodging in the shrubbery like crystals of salt in broccoli.

As for Alice, after our night together she crept back to the margins, the zone of silence. Sometimes it seemed to me that Lack had, after all, accepted her offer, and Alice had passed through to the other side. The part of her that mattered, anyway.

When I came home Thursday she spoke again, but this time my hopes didn't rise. The trail to my heart was growing cold.

"Something might have happened," she said.

"Probably something did," I said. I set my papers on the table.

"Something bad, I think."

"Tell me about it."

"Evan and Garth didn't come home last night."

"I noticed. Did you check with Cynthia Jalter? Or the blind school?"

"I called them both," she said.

"That's a lot of talking," I said. "Are you sure you really spoke to them? Or did you just dial and breathe heavily?"

"I asked," she said, ignoring me. "Nobody's seen them."

"They're capricious," I said. "They'll come wandering back any minute now, humming the latest pop tunes. They probably went out and got girlfriends and jobs."

Alice shook her head. "I can't find my key."

"What key?"

"The key to Lack's chamber." She stared at me, her eyes welling, her chin warping.

"What are you saying?"

"I don't know," she said, beginning to sob.

"Well, that's ridiculous. Braxia explained it to me. Lack won't take people."

Alice's tears stopped abruptly. "Braxia said that?"

"Yes." Actually, I wasn't sure he'd said that. But I let it stand.

"How does he know?"

"He knows. He's a physicist. It's probably some simple thing, some experiment he did. You could have done it, if you'd stuck with physics." I went on buttressing my lie. Why, I'm not sure. "So stop worrying about Evan and Garth. It's just a projection. You're obsessed with the idea that Lack would take someone else, after rejecting you."

Alice stared at me hollowly.

"I'll go find them and bring them back. You stay here."

I rebuttoned my coat and went out. I drove straight to the physics facility, of course.

There were students idling in the observation room, chatting about Lack, batting out theories. The Lack crowd, the groupies, making the scene. I hated them. I went to the door of the chamber.

"You can't go in there," said one of the students.

"Believe me, we've tried," said another.

"He'll eat you alive," said a third.

"Who?" I said.

"Professor De Tooth."

So De Tooth was still at it. My windup toy had turned out to be a perpetual-motion device. "I work with De Tooth," I said. "I put him onto Lack in the first place. These are my hours he's working with."

The first student shrugged. "Don't say we didn't warn you."

I turned the handle, went through the clean room, and into Lack's inner sanctum.

De Tooth was on the table, his stubby arms outstretched, the worn soles of his black shoes in the air, swimming his way toward Lack. His blond wig sat beside his open briefcase on a chair in the corner. When I entered the chamber he pushed himself backward off the table and onto his feet. I closed the door behind me. De Tooth twisted his disheveled suit back into place, smoothed down his tie, ran a pincer-like hand through his thin, gray hair, then scurried to retrieve his wig. Only after it was screwed back into place did he turn and face me.

"You too?" I said.

The small man turned bright red, fastened his lips together, and said nothing.

"Do what you like," I said. "I just need a few minutes alone with Lack. Then he's all yours. Or vice versa."

De Tooth picked up his briefcase and executed a militarily crisp pivot on the ball of one foot, to march past me to the door.

"And give me a sheet of paper and a pen while you're at it."

He escalated his eyebrows into his wig, fished in his briefcase for the paper and pen, then turned his back to me and disappeared.

I was alone with Lack.

I took De Tooth's paper and pen and pulled a chair up to Lack's table. The steel was still warm from the deconstructionist's body. I folded the paper into a series of lengths, creasing it between my fingernail and the hard surface of the table, then carefully tore it apart along the creases. I piled the strips into a bundle and ripped it in half to create a supply of cookie-fortune-sized slips. On the first slip I wrote:

DID YOU TAKE EVAN AND GARTH?

I slid it across the table, past Lack's lip. It rose on a cushion of air as I released it, then, fluttering down into Lack, vanished. I stood up and peered around the edges of the table. It was gone. Lack had taken the slip of paper. He'd found the question palatable. But what did it mean? I pulled another slip and wrote:

IF YOU TAKE THE SLIP DOES THAT MEAN YES?

I slid it across, into the gulf. The gulp. Crossing the line, it was snuffed out of existence. I still didn't know what it meant. Lack might like the paper, the ink, my handwriting. But it was possible we'd established a link, a common language. I was impatient for more answers, too impatient to quibble. I wrote:

ARE THEY STILL ALIVE?

I handed it across the line, where it was extinguished. Three in a row. We were talking. Lack had taken the blind men. He'd swallowed them up. And now he was confessing it to me. But they were still alive, wherever they were. Wherever it was that Lack led. Alive as Lack defined it, anyway. In a spell, I wrote:

WILL YOU EVER TAKE ALICE?

Fingers trembling, I pushed it across. It disappeared. This time I wanted to check again. I got out of my seat and went around the table. A part of me insisted that the slip—all four of the slips—should actually have swirled to the floor like maple-seed pods. But no. Nothing. I got down on my hands and knees, under the table. All I found was a single long strand of Alice's hair, left over from her self-scalping.

I went back to my seat, heart pounding. Lack would take Alice, he said. The worst possible news. At the same time, I was flattered by Lack's cooperation. I had a scoop. Lack was a Ouija board, and I was the medium. I felt possessive. This was the first time Lack had aimed his seductiveness at me directly. I understood Soft, and Braxia, and De Tooth, and even Alice, a little better.

I couldn't underestimate this enemy. The temptation I felt was proof of his power. I looked at the blond thread of hair in my hand. He'd already removed Alice from me, I reminded myself. And now he's promising to finish the job, to remove her from the world as well. I laid the hair aside, picked up the pen, and wrote:

DO YOU UNDERSTAND THAT SHE LOVES YOU?

I offered Lack the slip, and he took it. This time I didn't bother looking behind the table for something that wasn't there. The question was meaningful to him, and the answer was yes. He knew. Alice had managed to make her feelings known. I shuddered. I took another slip, and wrote:

ARE YOU WAITING FOR HER TO CHANGE?

Lack took that one, too. My worst fears confirmed. Lack was aware of her attempts to change herself for him, and he was judging her. So Braxia was wrong; Alice would be Lack's first reversal of policy, his first acceptance after refusal, after revision. Because she tried so hard. He was charmed, like a heartless mythological god with a mortal admirer. Imaginary bastard. I hated him. I jotted out:

DO YOU UNDERSTAND THAT I LOVE HER?

I pushed it across. In it went, engulfed, devoured. It was like he wanted to eat my love itself. Each answer was more cruel than the last. Holding my breath, I wrote:

IF YOU TAKE HER, WILL SHE BE HAPPY?

Lack sucked it away. I sat blinking, stymied. Was that better, or worse? Which answer was I looking for? Should I act selflessly now, urge her back up on the table? No. I'd guard that information jealously. Why had I been so stupid as to ask?

I picked up another slip. I had a thousand urgent questions. Then a vague suspicion crept over me. My pile of slips was half gone, and I still hadn't received a single no. Was I leading the witness?

I had to test him. I wrote:

WOULD YOU LIKE A LITTLE RED PARTY HAT?

The idiotic question was taken. Engulped. I picked up the blank slips that remained and hurled them toward Lack. As they fluttered chaotically across the line they each, in turn, were spirited silently away. Extinguished. Only one fell to the side, just missing the entrance. The rest were welcomed as gladly as my careful questions.

Lack was just a girl who can't say no. He liked freshly torn paper, or irregular rectangles. He liked fucking with my head. I picked up the slip that escaped, and wrote:

DO YOU UNDERSTAND THAT I HATE YOU?

I tossed it into Lack's maw as I got out of my seat. Bull's-eye, a perfect strike. I was nearly to the door before it fluttered past the end of the table and landed, with the lightest possible sound, on the floor.

31

I felt responsible for the blind men. It couldn't be Alice, not in her state. And Cynthia Jalter didn't live with them. They'd given me warning, too. I'd heard them yearn for a divorce from a reality that, despite their tabulations, always slipped through their grasping fingers.

I got back in my car and searched for them, pretending I didn't believe Lack. I followed the route of their walks across campus, and into town. I felt sure I'd turn a corner and see them, in their twin black suits, cocking their heads at a sound, or arguing the location of some phone booth or bus stop. But I didn't. The darker it got, the more possible it seemed that Lack was telling the truth. That he'd gobbled the blind men.

I exhausted the routes, but I kept on driving, repeating my path. I was mapping. It was like an incantation to bring them back.

Finally I drove back to the apartment. Alice was gone. I didn't care. I went in and turned on all the lights, trying to chase out the silence with light. I switched on the television and sat on the couch. No one came home. No moths were drawn to my little flame. The refrigerator hummed into activity, a life-support system for mildewed cottage cheese, stale muffins, encrusted, forgotten spreads. Outside, students walked the pathways, shattered by their attempts at last-minute term papers, pacing off the effects of powdery drugs consumed in the cause. I curled up on the couch and slept.

The apartment spilled over with sunlight. I was still alone, still on the couch. I looked at the clock. I'd slept all night and morning, through most of the last meeting of my freshman class.

I struggled back into my preworn clothing, my pretied shoes, ran to the anthropology building, and rushed upstairs to the airless classroom. Only one of my sixteen students remained. He sat alone at his desk, writing in his notebook with a ballpoint pen. He looked up, astonished at my arrival.

"Professor Engstrand."

"Angus."

"I'm almost done."

"Done with what? Where did they all go?"

He blinked twice. He looked frightened.

"Tell me what happened, Angus."

"We met and waited for you, sir. Sat in our places. But you

didn't come. No one said anything. Half an hour passed. Then someone suggested that your absence might represent some new form of final exam. Some arcane and menacing form, I believe those were the exact words. We laughed nervously at first. But one by one we opened our notebooks. Began attempting to answer the question you were posing. That's why it's a little unsettling to see you here, sir. I was almost finished. The others handed in their papers to the department secretary. May I ask you a question, sir?"

"Yes, Angus."

"Does this mean I failed?"

"No, Angus. There's no time limit. Hand it in when you're done."

"Thank you, sir. Also Professor Soft was here looking for you a little while ago."

"Thank you, Angus."

I went downstairs to the faculty lounge, looking for coffee and a pastry. The place was empty, designer aluminum chairs stacked in an awkward, helix-shaped tower. The professors were all out drinking quietly in off-campus bars, unable to wait for the end-term Christmas party. I went to the snack tray and fed on crumb cake and hot black coffee.

Soft hurried in, looking pinched. He saw me and exhaled through his nostrils.

"What's the matter?" I said.

He sighed. "Let's talk outside."

"I missed my class," I said, crumb cake clinging to my lip. "I need breakfast and a shower. I didn't sleep well."

"Let's talk outside."

I followed him out of the building, onto the lawn. The day

was bright, the winter rinsed out of the air by the insistent sunlight. Students were back out on the grass, lolling, as if after sex, their work finished or abandoned. Walking with Soft among them reminded me of our earlier talk, the day of our haircuts, the day Lack was named. We both needed haircuts again. It was only one of the many differences between that innocent, orderly time and now.

"What's the matter?"

"There's blood in the chamber."

I looked at Soft, hoping to see the signs that accompany cruel humor. Dancing eyes, et cetera. I didn't find any. His brow was knit.

"De Tooth," I suggested meekly.

"I've already located De Tooth." Soft's voice was reproving. "He's fine. It isn't his blood."

"But it's his shift. He's supposed to be down there. He's in charge."

"No it isn't. You haven't looked at your schedule." Soft pulled out his from his pocket, held it too close to my face. "It's Alice's shift as of midnight last night. De Tooth flies back to Belgium after tomorrow, for Christmas. We gave the winter break to Alice."

I started to panic, but I didn't let it show.

"And now there's blood in the chamber," he went on. "Lots of it, all over the table and the floor. Drips in the hallway. You were supposed to take care of this kind of thing, Philip. You were supposed to keep track of her shifts. I was counting on you."

Adrenalin sped through my tollgates without paying. When I spoke it came in a flood.

"Alice is a grown woman, Soft. She and I haven't been together for months. I can't tell her not to bleed. She's free to bleed if she wants. And I never made any specifically blood-related commitment to you, that I can recall. Anyway, you're assuming that it is Alice's blood, or blood or some simulation of blood that Alice for some reason distributed. We can't make that assumption."

"I'm not making any assumptions," said Soft defensively. "I'm making an observation. It looks like somebody committed a murder down there."

"Murders produce pints and pints of blood. The floor would be slippery with the blood of a whole person. When the police come upon the scene of a murder the rookies vomit, involuntarily. Did you involuntarily vomit? If not, I find it hard to believe that it resembled the scene of a murder, or at least the murder of a full-sized person."

"I didn't vomit," Soft confessed, looking bedazzled. He squinted into the sun, thinking. "It does look like somebody had a pretty serious accident down there, Philip. I don't mean to worry you."

"Oh, I'm not worried. Alice is her own woman. If I'm concerned at all it's in a friendly, interfaculty sort of way. I mean, she and I shared some good times. But there's no special worry."

"I didn't realize."

"What say you get back down there and wait around and make sure nobody, Alice or anyone else, gets back into the chamber? That might be important. I'll take a look around and see if I can scare up Alice, and when I do I'll give you a call. I'm sure it's just some little thing. We'll all have a good laugh over it at the party."

"What?" Soft looked punctured.

"The Christmas party. You're going, aren't you?" I chucked him on the shoulder. "Go back to the lab. I'll give you a call."

He nodded, his shoulders round with the weight of his confusion, and turned back toward the physics facility. I watched him go, my heart pounding. Disaster footage played on my mind's screen. As soon as he was out of sight I ran back to the apartment.

Alice's car was sitting in the driveway, idling, empty. The passenger seat was loaded with her clothes. There was a spot of blood on the carpet by the accelerator. Her keys dangled from the ignition, vibrating with the engine. I left the car running and went inside.

Alice was at the sink, splashing in the flow from the tap. A bloody heap of paper towels lay on the counter. She was hastily rewrapping a blood-soaked bandage around the base of her left thumb. I counted her fingers—they were all there.

She looked up at me, stricken, then grabbed the loose end of her bandage and furiously taped it down. She didn't want me to see her helpless. She'd obviously meant to get out before I found her.

"Alice," I said.

She looked at me like I was an entire roadblock of police. I tried to stay calm myself, to ignore the ring of crimson in the sink.

"Soft is worried," I said. "Apparently you left some kind of mess in the chamber."

"I cut myself."

She swirled water in the sink, rinsing away most of the blood. I stood and watched. She balled up the paper towels, clumsily, with her one good hand, and stuffed them into the garbage pail.

She met my eye, and I saw a hint of regret, as if the absurdity and pain of her situation, of our situation, had all of a sudden become plain to her. Then her gaze fell. She tugged at her bandage once to make sure it was secure, and went to the door.

"You're leaving," I said.

She nodded.

"Let me walk you to the car."

She climbed gingerly into the front seat, and tested her bandaged hand against the steering wheel. The wound was to the meat of her thumb. A bad injury for a driver. She tried to hide it from me, but I saw her wince.

I leaned in to her window. "You look terrible," I said.

Alice nodded. She pulled her lips together, fighting tears.

"You must be worried about Evan and Garth," I said.

She let her hands come away from the wheel, and crossed them in her lap, the wounded one resting on top.

"You're going to your parents' place?"

"I think so," she said. "I have to get farther away."

"From Lack, you mean."

"And you."

I was surprised. Alice blinked up at me, weakly defiant.

"You cut yourself," I said. When we spoke it was still in a lover's clipped code, tips standing in for icebergs.

"I made a mistake," she said.

"You gave part of yourself to Lack." It came out practically a whisper.

"A small part. I tried."

"He didn't take it, you mean."

She nodded.

I squinted up at the winter sky. It was a beautiful day. I felt dirty, unshaven, and hopeless.

Suddenly, idiotically, I realized I'd been counting on spending Christmas with Alice. A chink in my heart's pill-bug armor. I'd be hurt by her going away.

"You don't have to go," I said.

"I do."

"I understand," I said. "You feel bad about Evan and Garth. And everything that happened, your hand, me. But it doesn't mean you have to run away."

"For a while, Philip. I'm sorry."

I struggled for words. "You still love Lack, I guess."

She nodded.

A cold wind swept over the roof of the car, into my face. I coughed into my fist, and felt my stubbly chin and chapped lips against my hand.

"What you did down there is crazy, you know."

She nodded again, and ran her good right hand through her short hair, front to back. She had new mannerisms to go with her short hair.

"Are you okay?" I asked.

"It bleeds a lot," she said.

"Did you disinfect it?"

"Yes."

We fell silent. I wanted her bandage to come undone, her wound to bleed, so that she would need my help. I could carry her from the car, then come back, turn her key back out of the ignition, and pocket it.

"What should I tell Soft?" I said. I was stalling.

"About what?"

"I can't keep covering for you. It's too much. Questions are being asked. Soft said it looked like a murder. That's just one example. There's also Evan and Garth. You're dropping everything in my lap."

Alice looked at me sharply. "There is no more Evan and Garth," she said. "Nothing in your lap."

"Listen to you, you're jealous. Lack took someone else. That's what's behind these suicidal gestures, these elegiac departures. Jealousy."

"Don't, Philip."

"I just don't understand—"

How you can leave me, I almost finished. But I caught myself. Her car was running, and the chances were that in a minute or two I'd have to face myself, alone. So I put together another end for my sentence, one safely shallow and bitter.

"I don't understand why I go on making this so easy for you. Why I'm such a—what's it called? A doormat, that's it. Or doorman. Good morning, Ms. Coombs, watch your step, here's the void. When one word from me and the jig, as they say, is up. No more Alice and Lack."

That did it. Alice gripped the steering wheel, obviously fighting pain, and shifted the car into reverse. She pulsed her foot on the brake so the car rolled an inch away, as warning, then looked up at me one last time.

"Do what you have to do," she said.

She accelerated backward in a lurch out of the driveway, then shifted and sped away, leaving me standing there, less doormat or doorman than door, slammed.

I went inside and called Soft. I told him that I'd found Alice, that she was fine, and that she'd only accidentally cut herself in the chamber. I spread apologies like margarine. Soft seemed mollified. I hung up and went into the bathroom to shower and shave, to reorganize a presentable, inhabitable self. By the time I was done it was five-thirty. The day had leaked away. I heated a can of bean-and-bacon soup on the stove and ate it in silence, my mind vacant like a chewing cow's.

Then I found a dusty bottle of scotch, and poured myself a glass.

Two hours later I knocked on the door of the Melinda Fenderman Memorial Guest Apartment, where Braxia was staying. Students were partying in anarchic clusters, and the campus was like a darkened landscape lit by tribal bonfires.

Braxia opened the door.

"May I come in?" I said.

"Of course," said Braxia.

The Apartment was clean. The walls were all oak paneling, with a row of plaques noting the previous occupants. Braxia's was surely in preparation. His baggage was heaped in the foyer. I smelled bleach. The Italian physicist must have been scrubbing the fixtures when I knocked.

"I was just walking, and I saw the light on," I said.

"Welcome," he said.

Braxia was dressed in a white shirt, and black suit pants. The jacket was draped over the back of a chair in the living room. Every light in the apartment was on. Suddenly he looked like Manhattan Project newsreel footage. I saw him in black and white.

"You're packed," I said stupidly.

"My plane is tonight."

"What? You're missing the Christmas party?"

"I suppose. You? Or have you been there already?"

Did my breath stink of the scotch I'd been drinking? "I don't know if I'll go, actually. I was just out walking. The last night, you know. I like to feel it. Soak it up. And I wanted to talk to you."

Braxia smiled to himself, and led me into the middle of the tiny apartment. He sat on the couch and crossed his legs. I stood leaning against the back of an easy chair. The room was so bare I wondered if Braxia had packed up a few of the furnishings.

"Talk," said Braxia.

"You can't just go, like this," I said, surprising myself. "Soft isn't man enough to call you on it, but I am. What did you learn? Why are you leaving early? I'll pay your cab to wait while you talk to me. But I'm not leaving without some answers."

"About Lack. You think I have some answers for you."

"Yes."

He smiled again, demurely. "Okay, Mr. Engstrand. We will talk about Lack. What do you want to know?"

"How. Why. You said you'd solve it. You said you'd give me Alice back."

"Sit down, my dear fellow. You are making me nervous. I found out what I could from Lack. Lack is nothing. I am working on a larger problem now. I am sorry if I was no help with your Professor Alice. I forgot."

"That's your big theory? 'Lack is nothing'?"

He looked at me warily. "Okay, Mr. Engstrand. Sit down. You have an advantage over me: You have had a drink, and I have not. Now I will have a drink too. You want a drink? Have a drink with me, Mr. Engstrand."

I sat on the chair. Braxia went into the kitchen. I heard him easing ice cubes out of a tray. A minute later he reappeared with a pair of tall glasses, filled with orange juice.

"Vodka, you know, has the fewest impurities," he said. "And some vitamin C. Good for you."

I took a glass. He guzzled, I sipped.

"Okay," he said, smacking his lips. "A drink is good, for big talking. To talk to you about Lack I first have to talk to you about observer-triggered reality. Okay?"

I nodded.

"This is my life's work, Mr. Engstrand. Ah, I wish you spoke Italian. It's like this. Consciousness creates reality. Only when there is a mind to consider the world is there a world. Nothing before, except potential. Potential this, potential that. The creation event, the big bang—it was the creation of enormous potential, nothing more."

I was already lost. "You're saying there's no world where there isn't a mentality to consider a world."

"Yes."

"There's just a gap," I suggested. "A lack."

"Hah! Very good. Yes. A lack, exactly. A potential event horizon. Everything is only potential until consciousness wakes up and says, let me have a look. Take for example the big bang. We explore the history of the creation of our universe, so the big bang becomes real. But only because we investigate. Another example: There are subatomic particles as far as we are willing to look. We create them. Consciousness writes reality, in any direction it looks—past, future, big, small. Wherever we look we find reality forming in response."

"Why?"

"Ah, why. This is my life's work, Mr. Engstrand. I think there is a principle of conservation of reality. Reality is unwilling to fully exist without an observer. It can't be bothered. Why should it?"

"I can relate to that," I said.

"So, it's no simple thing, then, the creation of a universe. If consciousness is required to confirm the new reality, you have to provide the consciousness too. You can't make just a whole new universe full of reality, without making the commitment to look at it. You've done only half the job. That, my dear fellow, was Soft's mistake."

"Lack, you mean."

"Lack. My theory is the first good explanation for Lack. Listen. Soft creates a new universe, of potential reality. But no intelligence to fill it up. Fine, it collapses into nonreality. Perhaps someday consciousness will evolve, like here, and it will become real. A long slow road."

"Every universe has to wait for observers to evolve, you're saying."

"That's right. Except for Soft's. Soft's had a shortcut. Because it was created in Soft's lab. It is attached, it finds out, to a gigantic reservoir of nearby consciousness. Us. It thinks, I could exist if I hold on to this, you see? So it refuses to part with the mother universe. It is drawn to us, moth-to-flame-like. That is why it would not detach. That is how Lack was formed."

"So Lack is hungry for meaning. Awareness. It's his only hope."

"You could say that. He could wait for evolution, but that is a long time. Some more?" He pointed at his empty glass.

I looked down. My glass was empty too. Braxia took them and went into the kitchen. In another minute he was back with more.

"But what about the effects?" I said. "Lack's personality. His choosiness."

"Ah." He smiled into his glass.

"What do you mean, ah?"

"I lied to you just now, my dear fellow."

"Lied?"

"I did not forget about your friend Alice. She is central to my problems. She is the reason I have to pack up my team and—" He moved his arms, imitating airplane takeoff.

"What do you mean?" Was he about to reveal his own love for Alice? A passion that was driving him from the continent?

"It is hard to explain. Another theory."

"Tell me."

"Lack, in his hunger for consciousness, grabbed on too strong to one that was near by. Professor Alice, I think, was the one. Lack borrows her opinions and tastes. They make him imbalanced."

"What?"

He sighed and closed his eyes, as if he had to remember to be patient with me. "You see, Lack should be impartially hungry. But no. Instead he is making his stupid selections. Based on Professor Coombs, I think. Very unfortunate."

"You're saying Lack's personality is borrowed from Alice?"

"Yes."

"But then—"

Braxia wouldn't meet my eye. He drank instead. "You see why I lied to you, my dear fellow."

It was too much for me. My responses came in a crazy jumble. "I still don't understand why you have to leave," I said.

"This Lack is tainted by the persona he has adopted. Therefore he is useless. Professor Coombs' tastes are too limiting. Especially one in particular."

"Which one?"

"Against science. Against research, scientists, physics. I think she picked it up from you, and passed it on to Lack. You have this element in your personality, you will have to admit. And Alice adopted your prejudice, despite herself. Because she was so close to you. So now, Lack resists all attempts."

I was stupefied.

"So now I go back to Pisa." Braxia raised his drink, like he was making a toast. "I will make my own Lack. If I impart it with biases, they will be my own. Against the social sciences, perhaps. And American wines. Then we will see what can be done. Then we will accomplish some physics."

"You're going to repeat Soft's experiment?"

"Sure, why not? I think this Lack will close up soon, anyway. It can't stay open forever."

"It can't?"

"No. Violates the laws of physics. Hah!"

Braxia found this hilarious. He laughed obnoxiously. As he drank his face turned red, dispelling my black-and-white newsreel respect for him. I nursed my drink.

I wanted to deflate his smugness, but he was the only one who'd even claimed to have solved Lack. It was nothing to sneeze at. He was so sure of himself that he was leaving. Now Lack was no international prize, just a pothole malformed by subjectivity.

"Then Alice is in love with a reflection of herself," I said. "She's Narcissus."

"Sure," said Braxia. "But who isn't?"

"No, it's more than that," I said. "She was drawn to Lack from the beginning. So it's a combination of things. Her obsession with the void."

"Maybe. Here." Braxia jumped up, retrieved the vodka from the kitchen, and sloshed it into my glass undiluted. It combined with the residue of orange juice to form a blend resembling Tang, the drink of the astronauts.

"So Lack only takes what Alice likes," I said, still working it out in my simpleton way.

"I guess so. Hah! She didn't like me."

I looked up. "You only stuck in your hand," I said. "Lack takes whole things."

"No, my friend. I gave him the chance. I went on the table too. But I couldn't go in. Lack said no."

"What about Alice, then? If Lack won't take Alice herself—"

"So?" Braxia shrugged. "Alice does not approve of herself. Is not unprecedented, I think."

"So Lack knows things about Alice that she doesn't know herself. About her tastes. Lack could be used as a way of testing Alice's judgments, in an absolute sense. Even if she's denying the part of herself that feels that way—"

"Maybe. Who knows? Hah. Once we used scientists to learn more about physics. Now we use physics to learn more about the scientists! Forget it. Very inefficient. I'll go to Pisa and start over."

"Yes. Do that."

"Be happy, my dear fellow. The term is over. Drink up. Oh boy. You think they will let me on a plane like this?"

I didn't say anything. I was fathoms deep in my own sea.

Braxia's inane grin slipped away. "What's the matter?" he said. "You still love her? After this?"

"I still love her, Braxia."

"Okay. But you worry too much." Drunk, he was more perfunctory with his English. "Lack will close. You will have her back. If you want her."

"She doesn't love me anymore."

"You explain what I said, explain everything. Tell her my theories. Claim as your own. Then you will have her back."

"I don't want to tell her what you said."

"Okay, okay." He put down his glass and got off the couch. "Come here." He tugged at my sleeve. "Come." He led me to the bathroom door, which was backed with a mirror. "Look at yourself, Engstrand. You are a mess. It's been a long term, yes? Take yourself home now. Go to bed. You will feel better."

I looked. There stood a mess. The self-unmade man. Just a question of composure, though. I patted down my hair, practiced a smile. Outside was fresh air, elixir. I had things to do tonight, and the fresh air would help me.

But I wanted to conceal my intentions from Braxia. The party, and the destination beyond.

"So," he said, his point proven. He led me through the obstacle course of his luggage, to the door. "Go home. Think nice things. Have a dream. Forget about her, if only tonight. Think again in the morning."

"Yes," I said. "I'll think in the morning."

He unlocked the door, then pushed me through with a series of hearty slaps on the back. "Go home," he said, like he was talking to a wayward dog. "I see you later. We can have an international conference or something. Good-bye!"

"Okay," I said. "Good-bye."

The air was invigoratingly cold. My drunken eyes couldn't adjust to the darkness, but it didn't matter. I knew my way. I wobbled away from the porch, back toward my apartment. I wanted to mislead Braxia. I wasn't sure he knew where I lived, but I wasn't taking any chances. My legs buckled once, and I adjusted, compensated for the handicap. I was okay. I turned to see Braxia smiling at me from the door, a black smear in a blinding frame. He waved. I waved back. When I heard the door shut behind me I swerved, and headed, through the darkness, in the opposite direction. Toward the party.

34

"Philip! I was afraid you weren't coming. Have a drink."

It was Soft. Unaccountably gleeful, he grabbed my arm and led me to the makeshift bar. The room was already brimming, the air filled with a gabble of overlapping conversations that peaked and ebbed like automatic gunfire. I entered a maze of bobbing and ducking heads, with faces that crunched up with ironic anguish or jawed open wide with laughter, nostrils flaring, ears burning red, cigarettes and glasses and food shifted from orifices to holders and back again by subservient hands. Every head made up the maze, the remorseless consensual nightmare, and every head wandered through it, lost, frightened, alone.

Here I'd find a parting taste of the human world, perhaps even a voice to call me back from the brink. At the very least, a chance to stall.

"No," I said. "I've had a drink already."

"It's Christmas."

"Yes."

"Eggnog, Philip."

He handed me a plastic cup full of frothy nog and hollow cylindrical ice cubes. I tasted it, to be polite, and a surprising amount entered my mouth. Soft grinned, happy to see me drink. I grinned back, happy to see him happy.

"What's the good word?" I said.

"It's almost over."

"It *is* over."

"I don't mean the term." He grinned again, as if that were sufficient explanation. I wondered if I'd missed something in the din.

"What do you mean?" I said finally.

"Lack. He's closing up. Going away."

We were attacked by a costumed waitress with a tray of hors d'oeuvres, tiny wrinkled crackers spackled with phosphorescent pink mortar. She wore a dewy black nose. She was forced to carry the tray so high that her face appeared situated there itself, offered with the food. Soft turned and the tray came up under his chin. He reached around and guided a cracker into his mouth. With their chins each resting on the tray it looked like a sexual act, the pink smears surrogate tongues.

She turned to me. "No, thank you," I said. I ducked to open a route of escape for her tray. She jostled past us. I looked at Soft, who was chewing with his mouth open. "You were saying something about Lack."

"Yes," he said, swallowing. "Braxia told me this afternoon that he thought it would close up. Lack, that is. So I went down an hour ago and took some measurements. Sure enough. He's attenuating. I estimate another week or so."

He lifted his cup, beaming. I raised mine, and we drank.

"Attenuating," I said.

Soft nodded.

So Braxia was right. Lack would go away. It didn't change my plan, only made it more urgent and absolute. A shudder of fear went through me. I tipped my cup back, and drained away the last of my eggnog, then let a piece of ice slip into my mouth and sucked it clean of the sweet residue.

Soft finished his own nog and smiled at me dizzily, a smear of cream on his upper lip. It clearly wasn't his first glass. He was drunker than I was. And happier. Maybe that was the answer for now. I should be as drunk and happy as Soft.

"He's fabulous when he gets behind the wheel," came a voice out of the crowd. Then a roar of admiring laughter. I took Soft's cup away with mine, to get a refill. The bartender was one of my students. He filled the cups from a bowl, then made a show of splashing in an extra portion of rum from a concealed bottle. He winked, and I winked back. I was planning to fail him. He handed me the cups. They were too full to carry. I took a sip from the top of each and inadvertently slurped off the two mouthfuls of undiluted rum that floated there.

I brought them back to Soft. He smiled. I leaned in close to his pale, small face, and whispered, "Let's turn this party on its ear."

He raised his eyebrows, looking stricken. "I don't know how," he said.

"Just follow me."

"Okay."

"The key is women. To talk to women."

"Women."

"Yes, the largest possible group of women. The male personality expands in the company of women."

"Okay."

"Then once we've become large we can take on mixed groups, or just men. But only after we've expanded."

Soft nodded.

I stood on tiptoe and surveyed the party. It was thickening, becoming insoluble. There was a bustle at the door as a series of students entered costumed as sheep. A woman behind me whined, "Where? I can't even *see* him. How can I fuck him if I can't even *see* him?" Laughter bubbled up like clouds of smoke. The music switched to something relentless, the soundtrack to a robot's headache. A female literature professor danced in a corner, sweaty and self-absorbed, ringed by men in suits who clapped and cheered viciously. Her T-shirt read MY HEART IS FILLED WITH LOVE FOR ALL CREATURES. Smoke bubbled up like clouds of laughter. A strobe flickered briefly, reducing all movement to Keatonesque tableau. Bubbles smoked up like the laughter of clouds. I imagined the bobbing heads that made up the maze as balloons, tied to the floor by the strings of our bodies. Then I pictured them cut loose, to bob and roll, still laughing and smoking, along the surface of the ceiling.

Past Soft's shoulder I spotted a group of three women, standing, holding drinks, looking bored. I recognized one, the new professor of macroeconomics. She met my eye. I nodded, gulped, and smiled. I was still on tiptoe. I dropped down. Soft looked at me quizzically. "Don't look now," I said. "But right behind us. But ixnay on the ooklay."

Soft seemed baffled. I took his shoulder and turned him, so he broke into the group of women. "Here," I said. "You—" I waved my cup at the macroeconomist, my eye-contactee. She was thirtyish, with glasses that reflected bluish light. "I forgot your name," I said, making it sound like it was her fault.

"Umdoris Umfield," she said. Sounding like she accepted the blame.

"Umfield, of course. You're in economics."

"Field. Umright."

I leaned in, smiled dangerously. "I can't hear you," I said. "This is Professor Soft."

Field or Umfield took his hand and smiled. Her two companions shifted their weight back and forth, waiting either to be included, so that they could finally join the general gabbling and barking, or else be freed to wander the maze. The one facing Soft was tall and limber, almost knock-kneed. Her long blond hair fell around her face like a hospital bed-curtain. When Soft got too close the hair reached up, drawn by static electricity, and clung to the front of his turtleneck. The third woman, nearer to me, was shorter, and fat or thin according to how she stood, with black hair that was pulled into a knot, and a ring on every visible finger. She wore an orange scarf, not a decorative scarf, but a long, woolen skier's scarf. Blue eyeshadow. Her face was severe and enthralling.

"Work at the university?" I said, gesturing to include us all. Nog sloshed to the edge of my cup, almost over. I switched hands and tried again, but confused, I gestured a second time with the drink, my empty hand in my pocket.

"Athabasca," said the woman in the scarf. "Gender studies. And this is Ms. Anderfander, admissions."

"Gender, admissions," I said and nodded, avoiding their troubling, indistinct names. "This is Professor Soft, of hard sciences. And Professor Hard, of floppy, or more properly, flaccid sciences."

"I'm sorry?"

"Soft of hard. Hard of flaccid. The study of the flaccid. How do you do."

"You're not Professor Hard," said the woman in the scarf.

"Yes I am," said Soft.

"No, I mean you. You're not Hard. You're Engstrand. The one with Alice Coombs."

"Not anymore," I said. "That's ancient history."

"Do you teach ancient history?"

"No it *isn't,*" said the woman in the scarf. "Not from what I understand. You won't leave her alone, that's what I've heard."

"Where is Alice, anyway?" said Soft woozily. He made it sound like he'd finally worked up the nerve to pinch her ass.

"Oh, she's around here someplace," I lied. I stood on tiptoe again to mime a search. But then, victim of my own charade, I thought I saw her, slipping away through the maze. My heart lurched.

But the hair I'd spotted was long, and Alice's long hair was gone, chopped off. I was wrong.

I rejoined Soft and the women. "Who told you that?" I said. "Anyway, how do you know she wants to be left alone?"

The woman with the scarf gave me a frank and confident smile. "I know more than you think. I've become quite interested in Alice's story."

"How intensely horrible," I said. I looked to the others for help. Addlemaddle stood wobbling on her odd knees, listening attentively, her hair accumulating strand by strand on Soft's seemingly electromagnetic chest. Umfield was sipping at her drink patiently, her gaze distant. And Soft? He looked hopeless, his eyes spongy, his mouth limp.

"Yes, Alice's hegira is quite remarkable," said the woman with the scarf. "She's echoed a profound archetype, I think, with her silence. Her refusal. The language we use is constructed by males, you know, for male use. Female powerlessness is built in, it's intrinsic. So the language can't be reclaimed. To even speak it, as I am, is to employ the instrument of repression against myself. Understand?"

"Like Superman trying to build his house out of kryptonite," I suggested. I hoped it would throw her off stride.

"Right," she said, undaunted. "So Alice's silence is the paradigmatic feminist statement. A refusal to be co-opted."

"There's actually more to it than that," I said. "It's complicated."

"Lack, you mean."

"Yes, Lack. I didn't just talk Alice to death. Something else happened."

The scarf-woman nodded. "She fell in love with the Other. Do you want me to tell you what I think about Lack?"

"Well—"

"You'll like this," said Anglefangle to Soft in a stage whisper. As she leaned in she left more blond strands stuck to his chest.

"Lack is the Other," said the scarf-woman. Her nostrils flared to capitalize the O. "Just like Alice is the Other to you. It's natural to love the Other. By that I mean the mysterious, the silent, the withdrawn and enigmatic. The deep. It's a significant development, I think. The discovery of a lovable Other in Lack. A third gender. You ought to be more understanding."

"You're saying Alice is a pioneer," I suggested.

"She'll be remembered."

"She's a success."

"Well, yes."

"Let's find her," I said. "Let's find her and tell her. I think it's beautiful, what you said. We should tell her we understand."

I meant it. At that moment it seemed right and profound.

Soft gaped. I don't think he'd set out to create a third gender. A slush of drool and eggnog shone on his tongue. I fought the urge to whisper *swallow* in his ear.

"She doesn't want to hear it from you," said the scarf-woman, shaking her head. "You have to understand. It would be nothing but an imposition for you or me or anyone else to define Alice's experience according to some external standard. The more we intrude the more we risk closing off this entirely original experience she's had. When she's ready to use language she'll create her own vocabulary. She may speak in a tongue we don't recognize. But it's not up to us to decide."

"You're right, of course," I said, knowing it was my only chance. Anyway, I agreed with her now.

"I'm glad we got this time to talk."

"Yes."

We all smiled. Our packet of heads was happy now, normalized, made like the others around it, the tittering bunches. The women nodded and smiled. They would permit us to crawl away. I signaled to Soft, who grinned and raised his drink, lifting it into the bridge of hair that connected him to Ms. Abracadrabra. As he backed away, stripping the hair from his sweater, several strands slid across his arm and through the drink, falling back into place beaded with eggnog.

I grunted my way back to the bar, Soft at my heel. We found a spot there, an empty pocket, and lodged ourselves.

"That wasn't exactly what I had in mind," I said. I handed our cups to my student for refilling.

"Things went wrong?" said Soft.

"A little wrong, yes."

He wrinkled his brow. "I don't know if I agree one hundred percent with what she was saying. About Alice and Lack."

I handed him his cup. "I didn't believe a word of it," I said.

"Good. Because, really."

"Exactly. We're in complete agreement."

"Good, good."

"But she was very forceful," I said. "Very, uh, compelling."

"Yes," said Soft. He lowered his eyes, looking glum and intense. Overhead a gong sounded, and a horrific voice said, "Open, sesame!" Soft and I both drank furiously. We were alienated from each other, our plan to tip the party on its ear in tatters. My other plans loomed, dangerously close.

"Philip?"

"Yes?"

"Is it true what you said? That you and Alice have been separated for months? That it's ancient history?"

"Yes and no."

Soft nodded. Even drunk he was too polite to ask more. We stood in silence. I felt the alcohol numbing the flesh of my face, making my tongue fat and cloddish, blurring my vision. The music pounded through me from the floor. If I gritted my teeth I could feel the beat in my jaw. Possibly the music was eroding my teeth. I slackened my jaw to protect them.

"So," I said, changing the subject, sort of. "No more Lack."

"That's right." I'd reminded Soft of his happiness. He grinned.

"So you're rid of us now. The Lack people."

Soft frowned. "I didn't say that, Philip."

"No, it's true. We're always throwing ourselves at him. We're an embarrassment."

Soft crinkled up his face. He leaned in to whisper, but his voice warbled. And we swayed, our heads dipping together like a doo-wop group, the Satins or Royales. "To tell you the truth, Philip, I tried it myself. I don't know why. I guess I thought that since I created him I should be the one. He should take me. But it didn't work." He shrugged. "It doesn't matter. Soon it'll all be a bad dream."

"Braxia tried too," I said. I silently tried to count the table jumpers. "He told me. And De Tooth. I caught him at it."

Soft raised his eyebrows. Giggled. "I guess everybody's tried it."

"Yes."

This was quite funny, and we laughed for a good long time. Then Soft got hushed and conspiratorial again.

"Did you try?" he asked.

"Oh, yes," I lied.

We laughed a bit more, slapping at parts of our own and each other's bodies.

"Let's go find some more women," I said.

Soft's face reenacted Terran evolution, from early carbon stages up through Nobel Prize–winning physicists. "Okay," he said when he was finished. "But I just realized just now that I have to use the bathroom very badly. Very suddenly. I'm very sorry."

"No problem," I said. "Do what you do. Have to."

"Are you coming?"

"No, I'll here. Stay."

He handed me his drink and fled. I hoped he could find the bathroom in time. The way the room was bucking it wouldn't be easy. I had trouble even standing in one place, with only two legs for support. How flimsy they were. I recalled that mountain climbers never lifted more than one of four limbs from the earth. Always kept three planted. I wondered why this rule didn't apply generally. It was so reasonable. But I was hemmed in by people I didn't recognize. No one to hand a drink to, no way to free a third limb and apply this sensible, obvious rule.

I had no choice. I finished the smaller of the two drinks I held, slid the full cup into the empty one, then knelt to plant my free hand on the floor.

Much better. The floor was the way to go. It was cooler and quieter there, in the well of bodies. A whole new world. Dark and clever and strange. Nobody seemed to miss me, up above. Or if they did they were too polite to mention it.

How easy it was to disappear. Nothing to be afraid of.

Drink seekers swarmed around me, jostling me away from the bar, toward the undifferentiated middle of the party. I shuffled with them in a crouch, my knees bobbing in front of my chin, my drink held aloft like a flag, marking my column of space, my other hand on the floor, a rudder. The costumed waitress passed over me, her tray darkening my patch of sky. I saw now that she wore a fluffy tail. I followed her, scooting in my crouch, fixing her calves in my sights like a driver behind a distinctive truck on a dull highway. Then she dropped the empty tray to her side, nearly dashing it against my forehead, and slipped away. I was stranded. "The *point* about my dream," said a man above me, "is that every woman who kissed me and died went straight to *heaven.* Immortal life. The happy hunting ground."

I scooted off to an empty spot and drank the last of the eggnog. I wanted to stand again. I had things to do up there, an agenda. The party was supposed to be my farewell to the human realm. The floor was too marginal. I put the cup aside and rubbed my hands together, mixing dust and eggnog. The moment was right. I stood up. Or tried to. My knees unfolded horizontally, and I lurched onto my hands and knees, my face pressed into fishnet thighs. Female thighs, naked behind fishnet.

"Hello," someone said.

I'd catapulted myself into the midst of a group of tall, attractive women, judging by the legs. The newly formed emasculation department, possibly. I was on my hands and knees in what I could only call their midst.

There was one pair of pinstriped pants in the cage of legs otherwise made up of fishnet, sheen, or goose-pimpled, neatly shaved flesh. Pinstriped pants worn by vastly shorter legs. The waist of the pants was at the level of the women's knees. Thus a tiny man. Or massive women.

"Do you know him?" said a woman.

I stood, rising on my wobbly knees like the Indian rope trick. The pinstriped legs were Georges De Tooth. I towered over him. The women were a variety of ordinary sizes. They smiled and blinked at me. Students. A gaggle. De Tooth frowned at me from beneath his wig, eyes steely, jaw set. He was drinking something clear over ice.

"Georges," I said.

He flared his tiny nostrils. His entire face looked like it was machine-tooled. He lifted his drink to his lips and tipped it back, without opening his mouth. Maybe he just wanted to rinse his lips before speaking. I smiled. He didn't smile back. He got up on tiptoe and whispered, or mimed whispering, into the ear of the woman at his right. She laughed and rolled her eyes. Then, by some mysterious process, all the women began laughing and rolling their eyes, and then they all went away to another part of the room, leaving me alone with De Tooth.

"I'm Soft," I said. "With. He'll be anytime now. Along."

De Tooth didn't say anything, just stared. His eyes were firing a continuous stream of protons, neutrons, and positrons at me. I felt them spilling over the numb flesh of my face. It felt good, actually.

"Lack is closing up," I said, ordering the words carefully. "Did you hear?"

De Tooth almost smiled. He said nothing.

"Soft tried to go in too," I said. I figured De Tooth was angry at me for walking in on his own attempt. "Everybody tried. It just doesn't work, apparently." Then I remembered the blind men. I decided not to mention them. "It doesn't matter now, anyway, since he's closing up."

Nothing from De Tooth. He stared, holding his drink. Gnawing slightly behind his closed lips. As if on a pipe.

"So it's all over, I guess," I said. "The whole Lack thing. Or the whole Alice thing. I guess you could call it one of any other number of things. Any one of another. One of any other number. The Soft thing. The De Tooth thing. I guess nobody would call it the Engstrand thing. That's not right. Probably it's accurate to call it the Lack thing. Anyway, it's over."

De Tooth crossed his arms, his drink dangling underneath. He narrowed his eyes, studying me. The pipe was coming into focus now. There was definitely an imaginary pipe involved in his stance, his whole attitude.

"I've been taking a look at some other projects," I said. "Now that we've got this Lack thing off our plates. I've got a few ideas that might interest you. So we could fire up the old collaborative thing again."

Nothing from De Tooth. But I was rolling now.

"For instance, how about this: unifying the disciplines, the various modes of cognition, by *smashing thought itself* in the particle accelerator. Subjecting it to fantastic pressure and seeing what sort of basic components fly out of the collision. You and me, Georges. I think it could be big. Real big. I don't want to be the one to say it, Georges, but N.P., you know? N. Prize. You read me? Do I have to spell it out? N-o-b Prize, Georges. I think you know what I mean. You finish it, Georges. What are the missing letters?"

Stony silence. Dartlike eyes. Imaginary pipe.

"Okay, Georges. I get the picture. I see. You're going to do the easy thing. Stand back and watch while I self-destruct. This is fun for you, I guess. Being Mr. Big Guy. It's your revenge. You come to a party and surround yourself with titanic women and refuse to speak to me. All because I know your secret. I know that you climb up on tables and hurl yourself at voids."

Nothing.

"I'm sorry, Georges. God, I'm sorry. You have to forgive me. I'm not myself."

He studied me. The party flickered on around us, an alcoholic nightmare.

"I had a plan. I had it mapped out. I thought when I found someone like Alice I would know what to do. My plan was a failure, Georges. It didn't work."

De Tooth was the vortex of the party, the still, small presence at the center.

"I lied to you, Georges. I didn't try. Lack, I mean. I haven't yet. I don't know. He might take me. I want to find out while there's still time. Before he closes up. I have to know if she loves me."

The tiny man pursed his lips.

"I'm hinting at something dangerous, Georges. More than hinting. Aren't you going to try to stop me? This could be a cry for help. I'm not sure. I'm asking your opinion, Georges. Does it sound like I should be talked out of it? Talk me out of it, Georges."

Invisible clouds of imaginary pipe smoke rising up into the green and blue lights.

"You don't think he'll take me, do you? So you're not worried."

Nothing. Behind him, dancing had started, frenzied, primitive, spasmodic. The literature professor had taken off her T-shirt. Soft was talking to the tall, knock-kneed woman from admissions, his head enclosed in her hair.

"I'm not feeling well, Georges. I think I'll go outside and some fresh air. Get. Thanks for listening."

"My pleasure," said De Tooth. He put his left pinky into his ear and turned it slowly three times, like a third-base coach signaling for a steal. Then he marched away with tiny, metronome-precise steps. A vortex slipping away. Leaving me in charge. A mistake. I was less well-equipped in terms of silence and enigma. The larger chaos of the party matched the chaos inside me. I was a storm at the eye of the storm.

I stood teetering for a minute, almost sick. Then I stumbled through the crowd of dancers, to the door, and out under the tilt of stars, into the shockingly cold night.

Where, moving again and again through clouds of my own breath, I trekked up the frozen hill to the physics facility.

I used the elevator to descend.

The lights inside Lack's chamber were already on. They were always on. A stage always set, where nothing ever actually happened. There wasn't any sound, apart from a ringing in my ears and the hum of sleeping machines.

I shut the door behind me. Lack's table glowed in the spotlight, and my drunken eyes contributed a blurry halo. The room had been professionally cleaned. There was no sign of blood.

Lack was abandoned, I realized. Braxia was gone. The students were partying, or already headed home for Christmas. It was Alice's shift, but Alice had fled. Soft had turned his back. Soft was so happy Lack was vanishing that he was pretending it had already happened. Lack had been spoiled with attention, but now he would wither and die alone. I might be his last visitor.

I circled the table drunkenly, squinting into the glare. I was killing time. I think I expected Braxia to appear, the way he always did, and pull me away from the threshold. But Braxia was on a plane, over an ocean. Nobody was going to stop me. Nobody had even seen me leave the party.

Do what you have to do. Those were Alice's words.

I circled the table, hypnotizing myself. I was a question mark in orbit around an answer. I felt the urge to speak, but whom would I be addressing? Alice, or Lack? The two had canceled each other out, become one, then zero. There was nothing on the table, nothing at all, except it was a nothing that somehow included Alice and Lack, and a nothing that I wanted to include me, too. Lack was a hole that had sucked away my love by refusing to suck it away, a nullity. Now I wanted to be nullified.

Do what you have to do.

So I climbed up onto the table. It was so simple. I would be the first lover in history to receive an absolute answer, a *yes* or *no* notarized as cosmic fact. I gripped the sides of the table and vaulted up, first on my knees, then flat on my stomach. Or almost flat. I had an erection. It was rock-hard and almost insensate. Some part of me had mistaken this for a sexual event. I ignored it. I held the table tight and slid myself forward, until my weight was centered just inches from the line that signified Lack's boundary. I tucked my legs underneath my stomach, making myself a human bullet, and reached for the far edge of the table. Then I closed my eyes and pulled myself through, across the boundary, into Lack, and beyond the edge of the table, to tumble onto the floor of the chamber.

I landed on my hands, and flopped over backward, flat on my back, my head under the table. Like Wile E. Coyote tricked over the edge of a cliff in a defective Acme parachute. But there wasn't even a sound effect, or a cloud of dust. My impact went unrecorded. One small step for nothing, one giant leap for nobody. The floor was cold. The physics facility ignored me, humming. My erection slackened. I felt it untwist from my undershorts. My head rang. When I opened my eyes my visual field was spattered with phosphenes, like a bad action painting. I closed my eyes.

Do what you have to do.

So I passed out there on the floor in an alcoholic swoon, until morning.

I woke up and stumbled out of the chamber, into what should have been the observation room. Instead I walked into a new world.

I wasn't underground, for one thing. I was outdoors. The sky was orange, and cloudless. The buildings on the horizon were familiar but wrong. Skewed. Strange.

My foot sank into the earth. I looked down. The ground was ball bearings, heaped in drifts. Spread over the top was a tangle of green and yellow wool, which created the superficial impression of a lawn.

I turned. The door I'd passed through led out of the base of a gigantic onyx replica of the Statue of Liberty, which leaned on a drift of bearings, like a cooler on the beach. Through the doorway I saw Lack's table, where I'd spent the night.

I took another step and sank in to my ankles. When I lifted

my foot I dragged off a tangle of wool. I trudged away from the base of the oversize souvenir, leaving the door open behind me.

Ahead was the administration building, but it looked wrong. The building had been robbed of its color, texture, vitality. It looked like it had been reproduced in chewing gum.

I went closer. It wasn't chewing gum. It was clay. Unglazed terra-cotta. There weren't windows in the frames. Inside, the rooms were dark and empty. I put my hand on the wall. It was cool and chalky, perfectly smooth.

I waded on. I had to stop every few yards to clear my ankles of wool. I saw now that what I'd taken for buildings were facsimilies of the various campus structures. Some were made of clay, like the administration building, others of porcelain, or bowling-shoe leather, zigzagged with stitching. They rode the desert of ball bearings at various angles, leaning like the Tower of Pisa, or half-buried, or lying on their sides. They stretched on to the horizon in all directions. The hills above campus were gone. There wasn't any sun. The sky glowed as if some upper layer of the atmosphere were fluorescent.

I made my way to the side of a strawberry-scented wax replica of the Helen Neufkaller Arch. It wasn't in the right place. The facsimile campus didn't correspond to the original (if mine was the original). I'd have to mark a trail if I wanted to find my way back to Lack's chamber. I kicked at the wool to mark my spot here. My foot caught on something submerged in the bearings. I pulled it out. A pomegranate. I started groping around. I found a fountain pen, an eight ball, and an argyle sock. A boxed edition of Carroll's *The Hunting of the Snark*. At the base of a math-department building made out of glass ashtrays, I fished up a bunch of paper slips bearing my handwriting. They read, DO YOU UNDERSTAND THAT I LOVE HER?

A duck came hopping along over the bearings. At the sight of me it flapped its wings and quacked, then flew away.

I found a facsimile of my apartment, made of coiled bedsprings. The orange sky glowed through the wire. I looked inside. The structure was hollow. There weren't furnishings. There weren't even floors. In the center, on a heap of bearings, was the charred remains of a fire.

I went inside. The ashes were cool. I found the blackened spines of several copies of the Carroll, and a few burnt duck or chicken bones. I dug in the bearings near the fire, looking for clues. I found a Coke bottle, another pomegranate, and the key to my apartment.

I climbed out of the bedspring structure, and walked back out toward the Neufkaller Arch, which I still associated with the entrance to campus.

Braxia was right. The new universe was clinging to its parent reality. The results were poor. Lack was trying to make a world, but he couldn't get the parts. He'd manufactured a version of campus made only of the elements Alice found charming or harmless. Another example of rotten collaborative scholarship.

Publish or perish, I guess.

The most important thing was, Lack had taken *me.* I'd passed the Lack test, along with the ducks and pomegranates. Lack loved me. He'd taken my key, and my words, inscribed on slips of paper bearing my personal scissor marks. And now he'd taken Engstrand, in the flesh.

She loves me. She doesn't love me not.

I waded through the bearings, my heart beating. I just had to get back now, and tell her. Explain that she loved me, actually. Since she didn't seem to know.

I found the fountain that stood at the entrance to campus. It was made of crushed aluminum foil, which glinted brilliantly in the orange light. It was full of melted pistachio ice cream. The aluminum-foil cherub at the top gushed ice cream, green nuts dribbling one at a time from its lips.

Sleeping at the base of the fountain were dozens of identical peach-colored cats. A few were awake, and grooming themselves, or lapping at the ice cream. The cats were all fat, grizzled, and oblivious. It was B-84, the lab animal, photocopied into many cats by Lack. It didn't seem to care about its multiple selfhood. Cats don't look in mirrors.

I sat on the edge of the fountain and peeled a pomegranate. A few cats wandered over, half-interested, and rubbed against my ankles. I looked at the empty facsimilies against the orange sky. It was a beautiful ruin, a haunted Zen garden. Alice's, but she wasn't allowed to visit it herself. I'd tell her about it.

I sucked the fruit from a few pomegranate seeds, but my mouth was parched from drinking, and the acidity made my teeth hurt. I put the pomegranate on the side of the fountain. A few cats sniffed at it, but they were spoiled, weaned onto ice cream. I took a cat in my arms—picking at random, since there was no way to distinguish the original—and made my way back through the maze of facsimiles, to Lack's chamber.

Everything was as I'd left it. I went inside, put the cat on the table, and pushed it through. Then I climbed up onto the table and pulled myself across.

I tumbled into darkness. I landed on the familiar tile floor of the chamber, but the lights were out. Fortunately I didn't crush the cat. It must have scampered into a corner. I righted myself and squinted into the blackness, trying to find some hint of light.

There wasn't any. The darkness was hintless, perfect. The power in the building hadn't gone out, though. I could still hear the hum of the generators, and feel the floor vibrate slightly. It was just the lights.

I grappled my way past Lack's table, to the door of the chamber. The observation room was completely dark too. There wasn't even the hint of a form in the blackness. I held the door open for the cat, but I couldn't tell if it followed me out. I gave up, and left the door open. I reached out for the wall, and my hands found the panel of some instrument parked there. The buttons and knobs felt unexpectedly gigantic, and interesting. I'd feared these machines, before. Now I imagined I could learn to operate them by touch. I groped past them, to the door, and out into the curved hallway, expecting to find some light there.

The drought of light was absolute.

Keeping one hand on the smoothly pebbled wall of the corridor, I headed for the elevator. The wall dipped away from my hand—the phone booth, where I'd called for pizza. I lifted the receiver. Dial tone, incredibly loud, hugely reassuring. I'd never loved dial tone so well.

I slapped at my pockets. No coin. But the floppy cloth pockets were distracting. What an invention! I tore myself away from them, started for the elevator again.

The wall disappeared again. Another cubby. Water fountain. I twisted the handle, and put my hand in the flow. Water, cool as rain. No pistachios. I drank. It was delicious. I wiped my mouth with the ragged, staticky sleeve of my shirt—another remarkable sensation. Then I made my way through the dark to the elevator.

Inside, I pressed three or four buttons. The doors opened on different floors, all absolutely dark. I listened for signs of life, but there weren't any. No people, and no light. The building was alive though, humming, chortling, like an intestine. The sounds were comforting, and at the same time dangerously intense.

I knew I'd reached the lobby when I smelled the lawn, and tasted the breeze in the air. I wandered out of the elevator. Total darkness. I felt my way down the steps of the building, exploring with a probing foot. The pavement jumped to meet my shoes. I stepped out of the shade of the building and felt the heat of the sun beating down on my face. I stared up at it.

Nothing.

I was blind.

I couldn't even see the sun. All my other channels, though, were cranked up to levels that were almost painful. I heard a bird's wings beating in the air above me. My clothes were a collage of weights and textures, and I felt tiny impacts of pollen or pollution on my face. My ears were two echo chambers, reading soundscapes that warped madly if I turned my head even a fraction. My nose was attuned to rotting sewers, and distant lightning.

No human smells or sounds, though. I wasn't home yet. This was another abandoned place. Not my world. Not Alice's.

I stepped backward until I relocated the bottom step of the physics facility entrance. Using that as a landmark, I pointed myself across campus, to my apartment. The landscape felt huge, blown all out of proportion. But the objects I found—parking meters, bulletin boards, park benches—were normal-sized. They were islands in a sea, and I clung to them gratefully.

The final island in the series was my car. I knew it by a dent over the right taillight. I ran my hands over the car, like a game-show hostess fondling a prize.

Then I heard the voices.

I went up the porch steps, to the door. It was open. The voices were inside. The very familiar voices.

"Evan! Garth!" I said. "You're alive!"

The talk stopped. The silence was profound. I felt my way in through the door. Was I imagining things?

"Did you hear that?" said Garth wearily. "He says we're alive."

"I told you," said Evan. "You wouldn't listen."

"Huh," said Garth.

If I'd turned away, they probably would have returned to their bickering, and never thought twice about my appearance.

Since I stood in the doorway, they were forced to acknowledge me.

"Philip," said Evan.

"Evan," I said.

"Let's see. Do you still want to sleep on the couch?"

"What?"

"We can both sleep in the guest room, if you want. Or if you want the guest room we can both sleep out here, or in your room. I've been sleeping in your room, and Garth has been sleeping in the guest room. But I don't mind the couch. There's still plenty of room, unless Alice is coming."

"Is Alice coming?" said Garth.

"No," I said, dumbfounded.

"Okay," said Evan. "I'll take the couch."

"What if he wants the couch?" said Garth. "You should ask him. He always sleeps on the couch."

"It's okay," I said. I couldn't believe they were arguing, here. I wanted to scream, *I'm blind!*

"What's okay?" said Garth.

"Anything is fine," I said. "I'll sleep anywhere."

"You can have the couch if you want it," said Evan.

"He said anything is fine," said Garth.

I stayed only a few hours. The blind men were impossible now. They'd perfected themselves, a completely closed system, the loose ends tucked in, the channels to the outside shut down. They finally had the uninterrupted time they'd craved, to squabble or sulk in embittered silence. Dorms full of canned food to pillage. They could stop checking their watches.

I was inside their blindness. Lack had taken it and made another whole world. Here's what Braxia forgot to predict: Along with making a facsimile of our world, Lack had reproduced himself. His chamber, his table, and his hunger for reality. Like a Persian carpet maker, every world Lack made would have a flaw, a Lack of its own. And every Lack would want to make a world. Soft's experiment would never end. His vacuum bubble would expand forever, his breach would never heal.

Kits, cats, bags, wives, how many going to St. Ives?

It was hard to force Evan and Garth to notice my questions, but I learned a few things. They'd lived in the Dada-ready-made reality for about a week, wading through the ball bearings and wool, feeding on ice cream and barbecued duck. Then they'd climbed back over the table, into Lack, and emerged here, where they settled unquestioningly. Sure, they argued about whether they were alive or dead, whether they'd woken from a long dream or fallen into one, but they also argued over the location of specific fire hydrants, and about the chances of judging the amount of ink left in a ballpoint pen by weighing it in your hand. They were happy here. They were home.

I followed them back to the chamber. Now I knew how impressed to be by their ease and speed negotiating blind. They tapped efficiently with their canes, and I hurried along behind, tripping over roots and broken pavement. The supersensory effects weren't exactly a help. The world whirled around me, oversaturated and trippy. Evan and Garth squabbled, ignoring me. They weren't curious about my destination, and they didn't want to be rescued. I didn't press them. I wanted to go home. I wanted to see again. I wanted to tell Alice she loved me.

We went down in the elevator. Evan and Garth knew the way.

"Why did you do it?" I asked, suddenly curious.

"What?"

"Go into Lack."

"Huh," said Garth. "You tell him."

"Well," said Evan, "we did have the idea that we'd come through Lack and be able to see. We had that idea. I don't know why."

"You had the idea," said Garth.

"We can't see, of course," said Evan.

"Blind is blind," said Garth.

We left the elevator and walked down the curved hallway, to the chamber.

"Also, don't forget, we needed a place to stay," said Garth. "There was that aspect to it. We couldn't stay in your apartment forever. We looked and looked, but we couldn't find another place."

I opened the door to the chamber, and something brushed against my leg. The cat. I lifted it. It was purring. I put it into Evan's arms. It could catch blind mice and birds. And Evan and Garth might secretly need a third. I wasn't up to it, myself.

"Also, the radio," said Evan. "Tell him about the radio."

"Huh. I also broke your radio."

"He didn't want to have to tell you about it."

"Huh," said Garth. I pictured him rubbing at his chin with the end of his cane, grimacing, flaring his nostrils.

"Ironic, isn't it?" he said. "Here I am, telling you about it."

The chamber smelled of cat shit. I found the table and climbed up. My hands trembled as I gripped the cold metal. I tucked in my limbs like a frightened spider, and scooted across. Nothing. I tumbled across and onto the floor, and nothing was changed. I'd traveled nowhere.

I'd jostled the table on my way out. It didn't face Lack anymore. I'd missed.

I heard a mechanical gulp somewhere deep in the building. Evan and Garth going up in the elevator. Then the sounds died away, replaced by the rumbling of the machines that had been copied by Lack, and left here to rumble into entropy in the dark. The blind men had probably forgotten me already. But I might have to go slinking back. I pictured the three of us living together. I would come again and again to this room to slide across the table and fail to get home. Then I'd return, stumbling and blind, to make a bed on the copy of my couch.

I counted steps from the door of the chamber, trying to fix the original location of the table. Now, too late, I finally understood Evan and Garth's obsession with exact placement and distance. I envied their expertise.

I adjusted the table and climbed back up. More than my hands trembled now. I knelt like a dog on a veterinarian's table, quaking under some incomprehensible hand. My mouth dry, I pitched forward.

For a moment I thought nothing had changed.

It was still dark. I waited for my other senses to chime in. The cold floor, the hum of the generators, the faint smell of ammonia and coolant. Instead, the floor gaped away beneath me. I fell past the table. The room opened into a void.

My fall ended, but not with a landing. It ended when I realized that my sense of space was illusory. There wasn't any space, so there wasn't any fall.

There also wasn't anyone to be falling or not falling. I lacked, as I completed a quick inventory, legs or arms to swim or struggle with, mouth to scream with, nose, ears, etc.—i.e., the whole deal, works, caboodle. My body wasn't there.

Blindness, which had been a flat, two-dimensional thing, a sheet of black paper suspended between me and the world, had been folded into an origami model of reality, a model that filled and replaced the very thing on which it was based. The universe. The real. And me, too. I was not only in the void, I apparently *was* the void. And the void was me. There wasn't any Philip, wasn't any Engstrand. There wasn't any me. I'd solved the observer problem. Simply remove the observer, replace with nothing. Then, for good measure, remove the observed, replace that with nothing too. No observer, no observed, I drink, I fall down, no problem. Just a mind considering—ah, a hitch, here—itself.

I'd gotten rid of the problem of the observer only to open up the perhaps far knottier problem of the considerer.

Well, I'd have time to work it out, the problem I'd created. Plenty of time for thought. Time enough to demolish thought—as I'd proposed to De Tooth—in the miniature particle accelerator of my own disembodied consciousness.

I was wealthy with time. If it was right to say that this thing I had so much of was time. Perhaps it was space. If it was time it was certainly spacious time. Elbow room, as far as the nonexistent eye could see. And nary an elbow in the place. But it wasn't really time or space, I realized. It was nothing. I was wealthy with nothing.

Nothing, in great rolling waves, a vast, unchartable ocean of it.

Un-nothing too. The whole array of possible nothings.

No thing.

I found myself dwelling on it, the nothing, since there was so much of it, and so little of anything else. It became harder and harder to think about the things, or rather the memory of things. Those former, and now I saw, quite tenuous inhabitants of the vast, underlying nothing. The Lack thing, the Braxia thing, even the so-called Alice thing seemed far less interesting or pertinent than this nothing that pressed in on all sides. The nothing was tangible and timely. Real. Relevant. Thing, on the other hand, was impossible, fraudulent. I let it slip quietly away, thing. Easily done. Thing seemed embarrassed, chagrined. It fell away of its own accord. It knew to go. And it was so easy, afterward, to replace it, to fill in the small hole it left, with a bit of the spare nothing lying so close at hand.

The nothing. A nothing. Nothing.

I hummed to myself. Nothing, by Philip Nothing and the Nothings. Sung to the tune of Nothing. Nothing with a bullet. Ten weeks at the top of the nothing charts.

Nothing's greatest hits.

Supernothing. Hypernothing. Cryptonothing. Nothing ventured, nothing gained.

Goo goo ga joob.

I sent—and received—a nothing-gram. Some N-mail.

Then, unexpectedly, there came a variation in the nothing. A ripple, a flaw. A breach in the nothing. A small lack of nothing. Something. A sheet of paper, actually.

The edge of a sheet of paper was poking into the nothing. It was imminent and real. Undeniable. It poked right into the center of the nothing, which, because it wasn't anything, couldn't really compete, and was quickly displaced by the triumphantly real and distinct paper.

Since I was the nothing, and extended as far as the nothing did, and had the same center, the paper poked very directly into me, into my self-satisfied nothingness. The paper irked me. It was irritating. It itched. It ruined the nothing. Oh, if I had a choice between paper and nothing I would certainly choose nothing! Nothing was fuller. Nothing had depth and truth and gravity. But I wasn't being given the choice.

Then I noticed that the paper had something written on it.

DID YOU TAKE PHILIP?

Did you take Philip. I read it over and over, incredulous. Did, you, take, Philip. Unmistakable.

This piece of paper was trying to prod me into admitting, if only to myself, that there had been something called Philip once.

The question was meant for me, no doubt about that. I mean, here it was. It had been tossed over the transom of my nothing and had landed square in my eye. It wanted a reply.

Did I take Philip? Take how? Like a drug? Was I able to take him, withstand him, endure him? Well, barely. Or take away. Yes, that was it, of course. Did I take Philip *away*. So this was a message from the place I had been. Where, since I was here—despite, needless to say, being nothing here—I no longer was. Hey, I was nothing here, and I wasn't there! Nothing in both places! Delightful.

But the first place was protesting. Or at least making a polite inquiry. It deserved an answer.

Yes, I thought, trying it on for size. Sure. I suppose I did. He came with me when I left. Of course, at that point he was most of me, was in fact the whole of me, and I—the nothing speaking to you now—was just a hint or potentiality in him. A foreshadowing. But yes, I took him. Really, you could have him back, except I don't know where he's gone. I've lost him.

But take him? Sure. That was me.

Thinking it, my eye opened. My one wide eye, looking out into the chamber. The fluorescent fixture curved away overhead, the steel table peeled away underneath. Soft, in his lab coat and goggle-eyed glasses, peered in curiously at me as I made the paper disappear.

I'd replaced Lack at his spot on the table.

Soft compressed his lips, and slicked back a thatch of black hair that had fallen over his eyes. He backed away from my fish-eye window on the world and leaned over another slip of paper at the far end of the table. He was sweating like a schoolboy cheating on an exam. This was a clandestine visit. He was here against his own better counsel. He was afraid some colleague or janitor would catch him here, resorting to primitive, unscientific methods. He looked tired. He needed a haircut.

Eyes wide, he put down his pen, and pushed another slip forward with pinched fingers. The message rolled into view under my eye.

ARE YOU CLOSING UP NOW?

Am I closing up now.

Well, heck. Why not? I could see—if I hadn't known it already—that it was Soft's fondest wish. I saw it in the pensive corners of his mouth, saw it written into the lines of his brow. I, mere nothing, could make a being of flesh and blood happy. He just needed the right answer. So, okay. I'm closing up, sure. I took the paper out of his trembling hand. His rabbity eyes lit up with hope. He wanted to believe. Wanted Lack to go away, badly. I knew the feeling. I could empathize.

Happy now, Soft got up from the table. He swept the remaining slips into his pocket and snuck away. Leaving me alone, to stare through my porthole at the chamber, from this new vantage point. I'd never noticed the irregular line of foam insulation that sealed the top of the door frame, for instance, or the dangling, bare-copper cables protruding from the wall.

I would make Soft happy, I decided. I'd refuse everything. Let the students come and shoot particles in my eye. I'd say no forever. Let them shove objects across the table. I'd let them all flop over the edge. I'd leave every flavor untasted, leave every form, however nubile, unmolested. Soft and his students would establish, by process of elimination, that I'd closed up, set my jaw. I could see the press conference. It wouldn't be particularly well attended. The ends of things aren't news. Soft would have a gleam in his eye. He'd announce that the Lack era was over. The riddle is never to be answered. Soft would act sorry, but to anyone who knew him he'd appear relieved. He would promise a final report. It would be published quietly, during a lull in the academic year, in some marginal journal.

Then they would stop coming, I realized. I'd be forgotten. They'd put the chamber to some other use.

Maybe Soft's happiness would have to be sacrificed. Lack would bloom again. I'd yawn wide and swallow everything. A bobsled, a trench coat, a Spanish onion, a muffler, a spiny lobster, a footrest, a conveyor belt, a neon sign, a disposable jumpsuit, a pecan pie, a traffic island, a third baseman, a coal mine, a blizzard, a waterfall, a convention. I'd open my happy idiotic jaws wide and take all comers. Take laughter, take childhood, take love. I'd take all that and anything else. I'd show them all. Braxia, and Soft, and De Tooth, and especially Alice. I'd take all this stuff and make a world of it. I'd make a theme park, a garden of earthly delights. Soft would be like Old Man McGurkus, whose vacant lot was host to the mighty Circus McGurkus. He'd become involuntary St. Peter to this paradise. Forced by popular acclaim to open the gates and allow the thronging millions, the vast millions who would certainly assemble, the entry they demanded. And I'd admit them all, one by one. They'd bounce across the table gleefully, like people escaping a burning airplane on inflatable slides. I'd even take Cynthia Jalter, show her a coupling she'd never dreamed of. I'd depopulate the tired earth. All except Braxia, and Soft, and De Tooth. And especially Alice. I'd leave them there, alone together, staring into the invisible doorway, pining, embittered. Maybe then, one at a time, I'd relent, admit Braxia, then Soft, then finally De Tooth, but never, never—

At that moment the door to the chamber opened.

I expected Soft again, with another nervous question in block letters to offer me. But it wasn't Soft. It was Alice. She'd come back from wherever she'd been. Had she heard about my disappearance? I couldn't know. Maybe she'd just slipped onto campus and come straight here. She looked thin and tired. Her short hair was stiff, at odd angles from her head, as though she'd slept on it wet. Her eyes were rimmed with red. But her expression was calm. Her left hand was still heavily bandaged. I watched, hypnotized by her presence. She carefully and quietly closed the door behind her, then stepped up to the edge of the table and began to undress. She struggled at first, with her injured hand, to loosen the laces of her shoes, to undo the buttons of her shirt, to shrug out of her bra, but soon enough she stood completely naked in the chamber. The tendons in her neck were tensed, but her mouth was slightly open. Her breasts were goose-pimpled, nipples erect in the cool air. She put her bandaged hand onto the table and winced. Pulled it away. Slid up backward instead, lifting her buttocks, one, two, onto the cold table, then squirmed to face me, her damaged hand cradled beneath her, her good arm straining as she held herself up. I saw her eyes then, as she came across, and they were clear, and full of love.